Out of the Mist

ABOUT THE AUTHOR

Lynne, a Deacon lives in Devon and writes for ROOTS and Quiet Spaces. She is passionate about animal welfare and a life long Spurs fan. She has had a short story, prayers and poems published, but this is her first Novella.

OUT OF THE MIST

Lynne Chitty

Matador
9 Priory Business Park,
Wistow Road, Kibworth Beauchamp,
Leicestershire. LE8 0RX
Tel: 0116 279 2299
Email: books@troubador.co.uk
Web: www.troubador.co.uk/matador
Twitter: @matadorbooks

ISBN 978 1789013 535

British Library Cataloguing in Publication Data.
A catalogue record for this book is available from the British Library.

Printed on FSC accredited paper
Printed and bound in Great Britain by 4edge Limited
Typeset in 11pt Calibri by Troubador Publishing Ltd, Leicester, UK

Matador is an imprint of Troubador Publishing Ltd

For my family and friends with love and gratitude

ONE

Never had Eliza felt so lonely and so lost. Surrounded by the Isle of Skye's infinite beauty and with the gentle waves lapping at her feet she should have felt the joy of being alive pulse through her body. Instead, had tears been willing to come she would have wept enough to bring the waves up and over the small pier that was home to three scruffy fishing boats. Tears though had abandoned her a long time ago leaving in their wake an ache and a desolation that threatened to overwhelm and erode her of all she had once been. Steadily eating away at the very marrow of her surviving. Even robbing her of the energy she needed to get up from the rock on which she had been sitting. Making her way back to the hotel where she was staying would take all her strength. An overcoming of the pointlessness of existence that was slowly choking her quite simply seemed impossible.

She had always dreamed of visiting Skye, 'An t- Eilean' in Gaelic. The trip had sat proudly on top of her bucket list for over twenty years, ever since she had seen a photograph in a magazine at the hairdressers where her mum had her usual wash and blow dry. The Cuillin mountains had whispered to her from the tatty pages

1

and now aged forty six she had finally answered their call, taking the train from Gloucester to Kyle of Lochaish, via Edinburgh and Inverness. Then catching a single decker bus which took her across the Skye Bridge onto the island that felt like home. Until she got there.

A phone call as she stepped off the bus had drained her of everything that mattered.

He was back.

He had been released and was heading home.

He should have served twenty years. Instead seven years, and one hundred and forty one days later he was back in the lives he had so brutally trashed.

MARCUS

Marcus slammed the door behind him. "I'm home!" he called out laughing, knowing no-one would be pleased, but not caring. He owned the house, so dammit he would live in it. He knew there would be no open arms, no big hugs, but he had long ago decided to live life on his terms. His way. If there were casualties well so be it. Life was too short to be bothered with the trite little feelings of others. If you wanted it you took it. If you were afraid you didn't show it. If you got caught you got on with it, served your time and remoulded the pieces of your life on release. It was a good philosophy he thought. Self taught as well. Perhaps he should write a book!

His mother lay in her bed as she always did these days. He bent down, hesitated and then kissed her, shocked momentarily at how much she had aged and at how little

2

light there was left in her eyes. He thought he saw a flicker of recognition as she looked up at him. Fleeting though as she refocussed on the floral wallpaper which was as faded and as it was dated. Maybe he would decorate her room for her. Get him back into the swing of things before he lined up a few jobs and caught up with a few mates. The ones that weren't inside anyway. He checked his own room. Good, just as he had left it. Funny how big it seemed after the cell he had been in. He opened the window and breathed in the fresh air, shivering slightly then he headed back down the stairs and out again.

EDITH

Was she dreaming? She hardly knew these days or these nights whichever they were. Pain and a sort of vagueness that crept up on her like mist at sea had left her bereft of all but doubts and demons. Heavy boots coming up the stairs jolted her into reality.

He was back then. Back home. Back in her life.

She was not quite sure how long he had been away but knew that the silence of his absence had been a precious gift that she savoured every time her mind embraced a moment of clarity. He still smelt the same. His voice was as rough as it had always been and as he bent to kiss her if she could have moved with any sort of speed, she would have pulled away. As it was she had to endure the coarseness of his beard scratching her face like well used sandpaper. He seemed pleased with himself and filled the room as he always did with a sense of foreboding

3

and darkness she had never learned to live with. Maybe it was better that she was as she was. A cup of tea once in a while would be all he managed and if he didn't help her with it, it would just sit and go cold on the side. She smiled, inside at least. A cold cup of tea. How like one of those she was. What brand would she be she wondered and tried to remember all the makes of tea she had ever drunk... Yorkshire, Earl Grey, Co-Op's own and oh yes she would be a cup of Tetley's. Those jolly little cartoon men in the advert were fun weren't they! She went to laugh then fought back the tears that threatened to spill over and dribble down her face. It was a long time since anything like laughter had echoed around their house. Only taunts and threats and violence. Edith shuddered.

TWO

Eliza had hoped to have more time. She had hoped her mother would have been freed from the indignity of her condition. She had hoped he would go somewhere else. But like so many hopes their seeds never parted the soil. Or if they did, they were crushed by uncaring boots. There was a parable about seeds somewhere in the Gospels maybe she should look it up. Maybe...

Maybe was another word that she used a lot. It was code for never. Like hope was really synonymous with disappointment. She tried to remember when it was she had become so cynical and lost her belief in life. When had she given up on herself and God and whoever else there might be out there? The memory came storming back. The day, the date, the time almost doubling her over with its vehemence. She hadn't forgotten. Just buried the images as deep as she could. They never stayed in their tomb though. No one and nothing was strong enough to restrain them. They broke every chain she bound them with, gathering momentum like a ghastly hurricane as they tore through her afresh. She was beaten. She had tried to fight back as she had done the night it had happened. It was no good though. The memory had won.

MARCUS

Marcus had hoped to get out sooner but a combination of good behaviour and an avoidance of trouble had eventually convinced the powers that be that he was safe to send home. Maybe not the Full Monty of a reformed character but with his anger under control and a coping mechanism inculculated for life beyond his cell, there was hope. He hadn't always been this way. As a boy he had loved to keep rabbits, loved to see them prick up their ears and twitch their noses as he brought them the carrot tops Fred Rimmer gave him from his allotment. He'd like Fred. A bit slow maybe but great with his hands and anything to do with vegetables and flowers. Not like his dad who wouldn't have known a parsnip if it had hit him on the backside. Still, he shouldn't knock his old dad. He might not have lived life strictly by the rule book but he had put the house in Marcus' name before he died and left him his Harley Davidson too which had made him the envy of all his peers and some of his elders. It was quite neat really that his dad had died young when Marcus was only eighteen. Made him the man of the house and gave him a career and some boots to step into. Sometimes death came conveniently soon. Not for his mum though. Served her right really he thought. Miserable old cow. Don't know what his dad had seen in her. Felt sorry for her a bit but not much. No not much. She shouldn't have got in the way. It was her own fault. Course it was.

EDITH

Edith heard the door slam and unclenched her fists which she realised she had curled into a tight ball as soon as she had heard his voice. The carer would be here soon. At least she thought she would. Clara wasn't it in the evenings or was it Lara? Social services would probably review things now Marcus was back. Maybe she could go into a home and have pretty things around her and people to talk to and maybe even a television again. She wondered if Bruce Forsyth was still alive and whether Coronation Street was still on. Wouldn't she just love to get out of her bed and walk down to the Rovers Return if it was still called that and order a G & T and a packet of crisps. She tried to cut off her thoughts Where were they all coming from? She hadn't thought of anything for years or had she and forgotten? Exhausted from trying to remember she closed her eyes. Sometimes darkness was best. Except even in the darkness the pain in her fragile bones broke through and the leg they had taken nearly eight years ago still throbbed.

THREE

"Are you here for the half marathon?"

"I'm sorry." Eiza looked round startled by the mans voice coming from behind her, instantly regretting the decision to go over to the restaurant for a light supper. It had been a two fingers up gesture to the depression that had been seeping into her bones like the mist around the harbour. Now as the familiar exhaustion reclaimed the energy she had mustered, it felt reckless.

"Its the Skye Half Marathon in Portree on Saturday" he continued "and I wondered if you were here for that. Sorry if I made you jump."

Eliza looked at the man who had spoken and was surprised to see that he was much older than the voice had suggested. Steely grey hair and a well worn face gazed back at her expectantly through wire rimmed glasses. From the tracksuit he was wearing she assumed he was running the Half Marathon himself, although she wondered whether thirteen point one miles or whatever it was might not be a bit too much for him, though he was lean enough.

"No I'm not, sorry." she replied annoyed that she should have to apologise to someone she didn't know about something she wasn't interested in.

8

"No need to apologise." he said brightly. "Not everyones cup of tea. Love running myself, but can see how it can seem a bit mad if you haven't got the bug. My name's Pete by the way. Pete Hardy." He held out a hand for her to shake which she managed to do before blurting out

"I'm Eliza"

"Well Eliza I'll leave you in peace and hope you enjoy your meal. Food's excellent here. I come back every year."

Eliza heaved a huge sigh of relief that he hadn't insisted on joining her at the corner table by the window she had found. Then she felt instantly guilty and ungrateful, not to mention rather stupid. Why would he want to join her? She looked up in between studying the menu and saw that he was sharing a table with two younger women and a man. They all looked like they could be runners and were probably swapping training stories or tactics or whatever it was that runners talked about. For one horrible moment a huge wave of self pity threatened to swamp her. Struggling with a lump in her throat she ordered a feta salad, which she ate far too quickly to taste, before slipping back to her room, wishing she had the wings of the gull she had seen take off from the jetty. Where she would fly to though she didn't know.

MARCUS

"You're back then" a man in grey trousers and white shirt said as Marcus opened the door of the bookies.

9

"Seems like it" smiled Marcus as the betting shop manager came out from behind the counter to shake his hand. Marcus and Pat had an agreement that suited them both very well. No questions were asked and no harm came to the manager or his shop. In truth Pat had slept better while Marcus had been away but profits had gone down. A fact which his area manager never ceased to remind him of whenever he called in to check on things. So although he was surprised to see the big man back so soon, he wasn't altogether disappointed. A good summers takings might see him in line for a bonus. Which on top of the gifts Marcus threw his way once in a while could mean a holiday in Corfu rather than Cornwall. His wife might even stop moaning for once. Miracles did happen!

An hour later and thanks to a greyhound called Morning Glory, Marcus was £200 better off. She was in trap one and in her bright red coat she had led all the way as his contact had said she would. He had told a few blokes trap two was the one to back so the betting shop had done ok too. 'Nearly There' had manfully or doggedly should he say hung on to second place but as most blokes didn't back each way it wasn't enough for them to claim anything back. Marcus had made a big show of cursing and throwing his betting slip across the shop. Leading Pat to say he had missed his vocation and should be in Hollywood. He would have to give the punters a couple of winners in the next day or two but for now all was well in Marcus' world. There was nowhere else he would rather be.

EDITH

"Spoke to your son this morning" the carer said brightly as she helped Edith to the commode. "that must be nice for you having him back " Must it thought Edith Must it? She had always promised herself she wouldn't be bitter. But despite her best efforts bitternesses's oily presence had wormed its way into her insides and as soon as she had opened her eyes it had pounced. She didn't want him back. She didn't want him anywhere. Yes he'd been polite to her, and was out more than he was in. Yet still he filled the house. Every crevice, every corner. When he was out the silence deafened her and the waiting for the door to open again tormented her mind. Especially as she barely knew how long had passed. She had long since given up looking at her watch and she rarely listened to the radio. They were just cruel reminders of a world to which she no longer belonged.

Good manners were hard to defy though and she found herself meekly mumbling something pleasant to the cheery middle aged woman who was kindly brushing her hair. Though why she bothered Edith didn't know.

FOUR

ELIZA

Sleep had eluded her and as she tossed and turned, wide awake and as restless as the wind and sea outside her window, she had sunk deeper and deeper into a mire of despair from which she felt she would never escape. It was only four o'clock but reluctantly she got out of the bed which lay defeated as if an army of children had jumped up and down on it all night and looked in the mirror. She saw that she had aged. Within twenty four hours of hearing of Marcus' release the old haunted look had crept back into her eyes. She looked sixty. It wasn't fair she found herself saying to herself, Remembering how she had screamed those words at her mother everytime Marcus had ruined her games with his tantrums and temper. Sickness in the pit of her stomach robbed her of any appetite and a reluctance to face anyone threatened to keep her away from the restaurant and breakfast. But after a coffee which she sipped whilst looking out through the window at the sea filled darkness that gradually became light and a long hot bath. She mustered some courage and wrapping herself in her coat walked the short way across the gravelled courtyard to the main hotel. She was staying at the nineteenth century hotel Eilean Iarmain in

Sleat. The blurb she had read on the internet had called it 'A place to linger' It sounded perfect and she hadn't been disappointed. Eilean Iarmain had once been the busiest port in the south of Skye, with puffers coming in to the old stone pier and although those times were long gone, it more than lived up to its reputation. Everything about it, the setting, the atmosphere, the décor, all spoke of a place at peace with itself.

It was barely eight but the dining room was full and a genial buzz greeted her. Pete waved as he saw her enter and to her horror got up from his table. She was about to flee when she saw that he was merely going to grab some more fruit juice from the beautifully laid out buffet table at the side of the room. Even so, the man seemed incapable of not being friendly or cheerful and made his way over to her.

"Sleep alright?"

"Not really" she mumbled "You?"

"I always sleep well here" he said and to her intense irritation she found herself envying everything about him. His ease, his contentment. Even the fact that he was running a beast of a race in two days time.

"I recommend the porridge" he said. "They don't put puffins in it any more either" he joked.

"Puffins?" She said confused and once again exhausted.

"Took a trip to Dunvegan Castle on the other side of the island last time I was here and there was a stuffed puffin in one of the display cases. Apparently the folk of St Hilda used to catch puffins, ship them across to the castle, where they were put in huge vats of porridge to give it extra flavour."

He laughed and wandered away with his juice.

If she had little appetite before, the thought of puffin porridge completely finished her suffering stomach off and she just about made it to a table before putting her head in her hands. If only she could press a button and delete herself, like she could when she made a mistake on the computer. It had been a massive mistake to come here and an even greater mistake to think she could ever get away from the memories that irrevocably defined her.

The waitress who looked about twelve hovered nervously and when Eliza lifted her head she realised the poor girl must have been waiting for a while wondering what to do.

"Tea or coffee?" she asked in her melodic Scottish voice.

"Coffee please"

"Anything cooked?" the waitress continued as eager as she was youthful.

"No thanks"

"Well if you change your mind just let me know." she said smiling.

Thankfully she didn't add 'Have a nice day' or Eliza might have screamed.

The girl slipped away coming back a few minutes later with a coffee pot and a tiny jug of milk.

Eliza took a few sips and realised that in spite of everything she was actually hungry. She turned around and seeing that no one else was at the buffet table, crossed the room and chose some cereal and a croissant.

Pete must have been watching her because within seconds he was at her side again.

"Sorry about the puffin story" he said. "Sadly it is true but it was a bit insensitive and I can see you maybe aren't at your best just now, I just wanted to try to make you feel you belonged here and well made a hash of it. You looked a bit lost and my paternal instincts kicked in but totally out of order I really am very sorry. I could kick myself. "

Eliza looked up and could see the poor man was genuinely upset.

"It's fine" she said. "It's me who should apologise. I'm just not feeling very sociable at the moment." Yet as she said the words a longing for company, safe company overwhelmed her. "You all set for your race?" she asked trying to prolong the encounter.

Pete smiled realising it was her way of saying apology accepted and that he hadn't done any real damage.

"Maybe you would like to come? If you are still here and haven't got anything else planned. It's due to be nice on Saturday and there's a great atmosphere. We've got a mini bus going from here. No pressure but let me know if you'd like to."

She smiled and took her breakfast back to her now cold coffee. She wouldn't go but it was nice, really nice to be asked.

MARCUS

Marcus had hoped he would sleep better once he was home. But so far the nights had been as unending as the nights in his cell, where he had lain awake planning all the things he would do when he got out. He worked

15

hard at keeping the past at bay. What had happened had happened. No use going there. The landscape never changed and although as his counsellor had said, lessons could be learned. He preferred to endure the present and live for the future. The future was his favourite place on earth, full of possibilities. Dreams, plans, hopes, cascaded like a wonderful waterfall. They had made the long tedious hours of prison life bearable.

Thank God his cell mate Stuart didn't snore. He kept himself to himself and asked no questions which suited Marcus down to the ground. Poor old sod had been in nine years and at seventy one was well past his sell by date. Fair play to him though, seemed content enough and in no hurry to go back to life in the outside world. Not like Marcus, who had debts to collect and blokes to catch up with. Stu had been a good listener too. Sometimes Marcus had not been able to contain himself and had offloaded some stuff. Stu never batted an eyelid. Good sort of bloke. He really was.

Marcus looked in the mirror. A bit rough but nothing a good shave wouldn't cure. He'd always fancied himself as a bit of an Al Pacino, priding himself on his thick jet black hair. Something else he had his father to thank for. Mmm you'll do he said to himself and smiled.

EDITH

"Don't you look nice." The carer placed the hand held mirror in front of Ediths face. Edith winced. She didn't look nice. She didn't look nice at all. She looked old. Older than her dear old nan had ever looked and she had lived to be eighty three. Dutiful as ever though, she thanked the carer for helping her to wash her hair and she settled down to breakfast. She wondered how it was that her life had shrunk to the bedroom that she spent all her days in. It was her own fault really she decided. She could go downstairs. She could sit in the kitchen and watch the sparrows on the bird table like she had done before. Pottering about, baking, making trips into Taunton on the bus, going to church at Christmas with Eliza. A cloud passed over her thoughts and she was again engulfed by reality. Eliza was gone. Needed a break she had said. Would keep in touch. Touch. Beautiful word and yet how cruel touch could be, and how desperate when the only ones to touch you were strangers, just doing their jobs.

The door slammed. Marcus was going out early today. He didn't even call out a goodbye as he went. Just as well. The sound of his voice hurt her whole body. She woke up in the night sometimes convinced he was in her room. He never was, at least not physically. In her imagination though, he was nearly always there. Like a ghost who could never die. She thought about her own death a lot, especially when she couldn't sleep. She wasn't afraid. Not really. It would be much the same as now she thought but maybe with less pain and maybe even a bit of music? Was there music in heaven. Would she qualify to enter? She shivered. If only Eiza were there to read the psalms to her and to calm her nerves.

FIVE

ELIZA

Eliza sat in her room with a blanket around her shoulders staring out of the window at the view. The landscape seemed to change every few seconds. Mist dropped down and rose again. Clouds obscured and revealed. While all the time the mountains stood dark and beautiful. At one level, she couldn't help but feel better. They understood those mountains. They were calling to her soul as they had done all those years ago when she had seen that picture in the magazine. She had brought a camera but somehow she knew she could never capture them with it. They were living, breathing spiritual giants, friends even. She laughed. Yes, the mountains were her friends. She closed the curtain and grabbed her waterproof, suddenly energised. An hour later sitting on a rock in a little bay further along the coast she looked up again at the mountains as the water, happily settled in its daily rhythm of ebb and flow provided just enough sound to enrich the silence but was respectful enough to leave her space to think. If you could be depressed and content at the same time, then Eliza was just that. Nothing else existed except that moment. Past, future, they didn't matter. Nothing mattered except the joy of breathing in the stillness and the solidity of now. She wanted it to last for ever. She never wanted to move. She wanted to gradually evaporate and be drawn into the mist and herself become part of the landscape. Words from a psalm came into her head 'I will lift up mine eyes unto the hills. From whence cometh my help.' She wasn't sure if she still believed in God but as she spoke out the words she felt connected to someone or something. Though she wasn't sure who or what. A couple out walking their dog eventually broke the spell and as she got up ready to make her way back to the hotel, she whispered a thank you. The Mountains heard she was sure of that. As sure as she had ever been of anything.

MARCUS

Marcus closed the front door behind him. The street looked the same but the town had changed. Different shops, different faces. Even the The Golden Cockerel had changed hands and when he had walked in for a pie and a pint heads had turned towards him and then turned away. He had lived in Wellington all his life. On the Somerset, Devon border it did well for itself. It was set in the wide valley between the Brendon and Blackdown Hills, and had given its name to the famous 'Iron Duke', victor of the Battle of Waterloo. The 175ft column built on the scarp edge of the Blackdowns was erected in his honour. At night it was an illuminated landmark that could be seen for miles around. Had he known where Eliza was he might have been surprised to discover that there was a place named Waterloo on Skye. Sixteen hundred crofters had fought in the highland regiments and helped defeat Napoleon.

Wellington's growth and prosperity dated back to the 18th century when the Fox Family built their integrated woolen mill. Recent lottery grants had brought new facilities and added to the sense of community. It was a busy place and it was home or was supposed to be. One or two of the regular blokes had nodded, but he knew he wasn't welcome in the pub anymore and anger like an erupting volcano had threatened to tear through him. He had sat in the corner and watched Sky news feeling like a loser. Nobody treated him like that. Nobody. They'd get a brick through the window before the week was out.

The lunchtime crowd thinned out as the office nerds went back to their desks. He looked around again. George and H he knew but they were deliberately avoiding catching his eye. They'd pay for that. He suddenly felt old, weary even. It would be harder than he had thought to pick his life up again. His probation officer had warned him not to expect too much too soon. That he would have to work hard to gain peoples trust again. He'd thought she was talking a load of crap. He'd thought people would understand about what happened and just make way for him to ease himself back into his old routine. What if he couldn't get any work? For a moment his self confidence threatened to walk out on him too. He'd manage. He'd got a stash tucked away. The old geezers in the bookies knew where their bread was buttered. He'd just have to make things happen. Shame Fred Rimmer wasn't still alive. He could have gone down to the allotment and watched him tend to his veg. Always calmed him that did. Been dead fifteen years though or was it twenty?. Bloody time kept marching on slipping through his fingers however hard he tried to hold on to it. On impulse he put a pound in the fruit machine on his way out of the pub. He punched his fist in the air as he won a tenner, then doubled it up and up. He made an exaggerated show of collecting his winnings and walked out with his normal air of arrogance restored. He'd be alright, at least Lady Luck was still on speaking terms. The rest could go to hell. If the blokes he'd met in prison hadn't taken all the seats that was. If overpopulation on earth was a problem it must be bedlam down there. He fingered the coins in his pocket and smirked. Friday night he would trash the place.

EDITH

For once Edith had slept. Or at least she thought she had. She woke with a sense of peace and vaguely remembered dreaming about the sea. She'd been paddling and a dog had been running round her excitedly splashing and shaking, sending droplets of water in every direction. The best thing she remembered though was that she had been happy. Laughing, jumping up and down in the water at the sheer joy of being alive. Danny. That was the name of her first dog. A black Labrador he was and as placid as the day was long. His only vice was greed! Dustbin was his nickname, his favourite food were squashed chips that he ate off the pavement in Canvey Island where they had gone on holiday. Her, her brother Nick and their parents. All long since gone. If only she'd known they were going to be the best days of her life she might have tried to make them last. Instead, she took them for granted. Until one by one Danny first, then Nick in a motor bike accident when he was only eighteen , then mum who had never got over the shock, and finally her dad had all left her to fend for herself. She might have been twenty- two but she hadn't been ready to be an orphan. Stanley, Elizas father had come into her life not long after. He hadn't exactly swept her off her feet but he had talked the talk and one evening in the back of his car, Eliza had been conceived. He'd done the right thing and married her but in his heart he had resented her and the child, blaming them for a life that had never lived up to his expectations. He had finally left when Eliza was eight and moved to Blackpool if the solitary postcard they had received was to be believed. Technically she was still Mrs Stanley Harris. If he was still alive that was. She stopped to think how old he would be. If she was sixty nine. God was that all she was? Shocked she sat up and saw herself for the first time as still being young enough to have a life. She fought to hold on to this clarity, but gradually the exhaustion and the despair forced her eyes to close. Stanleys face came into her mind. He had been five years older than her. He would be seventy four. The bathroom door slammed and she let go of everything and retreated further into the safety of the darkness of the nothingness that got her through each day. Marcus had never been a morning person. Not even as a boy. Getting him to school had been a nightmare. Nightmare. The word frightened her and she trembled, suddenly very cold.

SIX

ELIZA

Eliza had started writing again. She'd never been terribly good, so it had been no great loss to the world when she had stopped. However, she had missed it. She loved poetry best. Painting pictures with words. Mary Oliver was her favourite poet and she longed to write just one poem as good as the New Zealand writer who seemed incapable of penning anything other than verses of beauty and soul. Her own poetry though mediocre at best, had filled her journals. They were to her like a photo album. Each poem, telling a story. Capturing a moment. Bringing back sounds and smells. Voices, feelings. Even sometimes, the silence.

Her counsellor had encouraged her to write about the trauma. It might help you journey through the experience she had said somewhat too enthusiastically for Elizas comfort, making her retreat further inside. She knew what had happened was beyond words. All she had been able to do on the paper her counsellor had given her was to draw black lines. She had covered the paper. Dark, thick black zig-zags crossing from corner to corner, deeper and deeper until she had broken the lead and blunted the pencil. She knew that Margaret, the lady she had been sent to see had been disappointed and even a bit shocked that she hadn't been able to put even a few words together. She was a lovely woman. Fiftyish with ginger curls and a vibrant face and Eliza had longed to please her. She felt guilty for failing. For not being able to offer her some encouragement that she was making progress. What happened she wondered when counsellors patients didn't come through. When the pain overwhelmed them and they ended their lives. They would need counselling themselves she supposed. At the time she had felt angry for feeling a sense of responsibility towards the woman who was being paid to help her. It was one extra burden, as if she didn't have enough,

In the end after twelve excruciating weeks. Eliza had stopped going. She sent Margaret a note explaining that it wasn't her fault. She just couldn't help her. She'd added that she shouldn't feel bad and that she was deeply grateful for her efforts. Ultimately it was the disappointment that Eliza couldn't cope with. Each Wednesday, between eleven thirty and twelve twenty, she had a chance to talk. To be listened to and in spite of everything, each Wednesday she got her hopes up. It gave her routine when everything else had fallen apart. It gave her something to aim for and she believed or tried to believe that Margaret could take away the pain and make everything alright. It had been a childish hope and each Wednesday she had left the clinic more depressed than ever. What was meant to be a lifeline had been dragging her deeper and deeper into the waters of misery. She just couldn't go on any more.

It had been six years since she had written that letter to Margaret and now she had finally written a poem.

ON SKYE BEACH

A blanket of stones, like
Bones, weathered and aged,
Covered and deserted by the ebb and flow
of the blood of the sea.
Smaller ones
Like speckled eggs
In a vast nest
Patrolled by pigeons and gulls
And trampled on by feet like mine
In shoes
So unsuitable.
And all the while the sea,
Gentle today
Caresses my thoughts
With its gush and trickle
And music
And I remember
You.

MARCUS

Marcus sat in the cafe reading the paper. The remains of
his egg and bacon were sprawled across the plate as he
took in the headlines. He loved this time of day. He felt
unrushed and there was almost something sacred about
the rhythm of walking to the cafe, ordering a full English
and sitting by the window with his paper. The day, as yet
unspoilt, lay ahead of him. He got out his pen and put

a cross by the horses he would bet on later. A niggle of uncertainty fluttered in his guts but he swilled down the last of his tea and tried to make plans. He couldn't live off his winnings. They weren't machines those horses and sometimes for no reason at all they just didn't perform. He'd need to get back to painting and decorating soon. The three thousand quid he'd stashed before he'd gone inside wouldn't last for ever and he had no intention of going without. Life was too bloody short for that. He'd make a couple of calls and see if he could get Ant and Dec interested in teaming up with him again. Ant was into antiques and worked the auction houses. Dec, an estate agent, got him decorating jobs in houses where the elderly owners were looking to downsize. Marcus took along his camera and took photos of anything he though might sell and then in casual conversations with the householders, usually women, he encouraged them to send the paintings, or vases, or furniture or whatever it might be to auction. It made sense he'd tell them. You won't have space for everything in your new place, so why not get a good price for them now? He'd hit the jackpot not long before he'd gone down. One silly cow had asked him if he would sell her jewellery too. Which he did. She had been thrilled with the four hundred quid he had given her. Not knowing that he, Ant and Dec had made a grand apiece. Did he feel bad? No why should he? It wasn't stealing, not as such. He always backed off it the owners didn't want to sell. He was offering a service and it was only right that he took a cut.

Anyway he would need to get up and running again. Get all his stuff out the garage and a few legitimate jobs under his belt. In the mean time he fancied 'On Your Bike' in the 2.15 at Epsom. He'd go and see Pat at the bookies.

EDITH

The carer Beth, had been chatty this morning. Going on about her family. Her words mostly washed over Ediths head. She didn't want to hear about their lives and she didn't want them in her life. She had mumbled a few yeses and oh dears as the younger woman had explained how her husband had gone on a fishing trip with his mates leaving her to look after the eight year old twins on her own. When she had gone, Edith had for once stayed in her chair. Bed felt a much safer place to be but as she sat with her as yet unopened book beside her, she again found herself thinking about the past.

She hadn't loved either of the men she had children by. They had just been there. With Stanley, she had lost her innocence. With Richard, Marcus' dad, she had lost her way, her identity. Then finally her leg. Though she couldn't blame Richard for that he'd died long before.

She didn't really blame anyone for her life. Except herself. Her bad luck. Her bad choices. Her weakness and then her fear had colluded with the emergence of Marcus bullying behaviour and now it was all too late. She'd wanted to be a librarian as a young girl. Working among books day in day out seemed a heavenly occupation. In fact it had been Eliza who had chosen that as a career. Edith smiled. Ever since she could read Eliza had devoured books like there was no tomorrow. Edith had harboured

27

a secret hope that one day her daughter would write a book of her own. She had the ability, all her teachers had said she had a way with words. They also said she was rather quiet and solitary, but didn't that go with writing? She hadn't seemed to need friends, choosing instead to share the lives of the characters in her books. I've travelled the world she'd say, excited by the latest adventures of Dervla Murphy who she adored. In truth, she'd never been further than London but she didn't seem to mind. Oh Eliza. Edith sighed. She would get back into bed after all. Reaching for her stick she hauled herself back beneath the sheets. At least Beth had changed them before she left.

SEVEN

ELIZA

The sun, like the star of a show had made a spectacular entrance just before mid day and the sea was sparkling in a million places. It was as if a great wizard had waved a wand over the water and invited it to dance. It was truly magical and Eliza couldn't help but smile. She was in wonderland, a child who nothing could hurt. The gulls equally entranced soared lazily overhead. Then it happened, a seal popped its head up out of the water. Eliza gasped and willed the creature to stay, but it was gone again in a moment. As hard as Eliza looked she couldn't spot the black head and she had to be content with the memory. Fleeting as it had been, it would sustain her. She had seen a seal. Her favourite of all animals. Warm and ridiculously excited she went to take off her pale blue jumper, but then she stopped herself.

It was ironic that the only visible wounds from the attack that she bore were those she had inflicted on herself. For months her razor blade had been her greatest friend and her greatest security. Looking back she wasn't sure if she had been trying to cut Marcus' presence from her body or whether it was simply about the pain. A pain that she couldn't cope with, however deep she cut. A pain she couldn't reach or name or overcome. The scars though not raw were still visible on her arms and she still wore long sleeved shirts and blouses or jumpers whatever the temperature. She had read a few months ago that self - harm was on the increase and she could understand why. But it wasn't the right way to cope. It didn't change anything in the long term and sometimes when she looked at her body she could barely believe what she had done to herself. At least it was talked about now and people could get help. Help. A strange word. 'To come to the aid of'. 'To give assistance to.' Her mother had tried with terrifying consequences. And since then, her doctor, her counsellor, her work colleagues, they had all tried to help. One by one she had pushed them away. Withdrawing into a place where no one could reach her. Until gradually, scarred, underweight and aged, she had emerged from her isolation and tried to begin again.

Moving away from her mother had been the hardest thing she had ever done. She had held her mums hand as she explained she needed to make a break, a fresh start. To get away from the memories that were in every room and the pity that was in the eyes of everyone she knew. I'm going to Gloucester she had said. The puzzlement in her mothers eyes had nearly broken her but she had kissed her on the forehead and ten days later walked away.

She hadn't exactly stuck a pin in a map of the British Isles, for a while she had wondered about going to Blackpool to track her father down if he was still there. But in the end she'd gone for convenience and the work.

Gloucester library had a job going. She had gone for the interview got the post and rented a bed sit by the park. It wasn't cheerful but it was cheap and she'd been able to pay for a carer/companion for her mother and even save a bit too. Resulting in the pilgrimage to Skye.

Eliza looked again at the place where the seal had been. She boldly laid her jumper down by her bag and ate the packed lunch she had ordered from the hotel. The past was like the tide she thought. You could never stop it coming in, but it went out too. Not for long maybe, but it inched away from the shore of the present, leaving pools of possibilities to be explored.She got out her notebook

THE POOL

I saw a pool whose water was deep blue
But couldn't reach it I ached in longing,
Ashamed
Tears trickled down my face,
and then as I watched, they joined the pool,
they became the pool
And like the mountains that surrounded the shore,
I held my head up high
A voice said
'Come,
Come bathe in the pool of tears whose name is healing

And I stood, wondering
If I dare step in.

Eliza scribbled out the words. Sentimental nonsense she thought, as she looked up at the mountains which even in the June sun were stark and foreboding. In that moment though, she wasn't afraid.

MARCUS

Things were looking up. The sun was shining, Desert Superstar had won and he had got a great new jacket in the St James' Hospice shop for a fiver. Would have cost over a hundred quid new. Ted Baker stuff didn't come cheap. He wondered if the previous owner had snuffed it. Or maybe he was so loaded he bought a jacket every week and only wore it once. Not many loaded people in Wellington but there were plenty with enough for Marcus to be interested in. He was meeting Ant later for lunch. He'd seemed a bit reluctant at first but a few choice words and gentle, and then not so gentle reminders of their previous collaboration soon brought him round. No one but no one said No to Marcus. For a second he remembered Eliza's piercing scream but buried the thought as soon as it surfaced. It had been her fault. Not his. He hadn't been surprised to find that she had moved away. If the truth was known he was glad. Hadn't seen her since that day in court when he'd been sentenced. She had always thought she was better than him. Head in her bloody books and fancying herself as a writer. Waste of space daydreamer and not even pretty. Gust of wind would blow her over and with her short straight hair and shapeless body he wasn't surprised that she never went out. What a waste of time that would have been. She was a joke. Now Ellen, who he was seeing later that night. Now she was what he called a woman. They understood each other. No commitments. No questions. Just sex.

He had no hankering to be married. He couldn't be faithful if his life depended on it. Sometimes he thought about fathering a kid just to keep his name going. Knowing his luck though he'd get a daughter and he didn't want one of those. No way. His thoughts turned again to Frank Rimmer. He'd had two daughters and been so proud of them. Which was odd as neither of them amounted to much. Both married young and moved away. They were good people though. Maybe that was what made Frank proud. Nobody would ever be proud of me Marcus thought. Still he did what he had to do and with that thought in his head he stopped at the newsagents for some fags.

EDITH

Filthy habit smoking, but neither Marcus, nor his father before him had respected her wishes and both smoked in the house. Every time Marcus came in, he brought with him the sickening smell of stale sweat and cigarettes. How had she grown to hate him? Her own son. The boy she had cried over, worried about, adored and now detested. When had the gentle boy she loved become so obnoxious and so angry? How had it happened? She racked her brain to try and remember the first time his temper had frightened her. Could she have done more?

33

She had always blamed Richard. He had derided his son for his love of animals and called him a nancy boy for crying when Digger, their Jack Russell had died. She had tried to stand up for Marcus but that had made it worse. Mummys boy and much more had been thrown in both their faces. Richard had grown up fast. As an evacuee he had spent long periods away from London where he had been born and he learned to fend for himself. He ran away when the war ended and made a life for himself. Eventually moving to Wellington where they had met. She knew he had fingers in lots of pies and that he had been forced to leave London in a hurry but all she had wanted was a proper home for herself and Eliza. So she overlooked that which she didn't approve of, and didn't ask questions. She bore Marcus and when Richard had collapsed and died one October morning on his way to the papershop, she had settled into widowhood.

She hadn't been surprised that he had left the house to Marcus.What had shocked her was the amount of cash and jewellery she had found in a box behind his bureau. Worried that Marcus would discover it she had hidden it under her nighties in her dressing table. It had taken her ten months to pluck up the courage to count the money which had amount to one thousand, eight hundred and thirty pounds. The jewellery she had sent to auction and worried day and night that there would be a knock on her door from the police asking her to account for being in the possession of stolen goods. The knock never came, though a cheque for nine hundred and seventy pounds did.

Opening a building society account had been nerve wracking but ultimately thrilling. It was her money now. She did still worry about where it had come from and whether anyone was grieving for the jewellery but not enough to do anything about it. It was all too late anyway. She supposed she was as bad as Richard really. It was her security in case Marcus ever threw her out. Or more likely if he lost the house gambling or in some deal or whatever it might be Three thousand pounds wasn't much but it was hers. Not much else was. Even her mind had distanced itself and no longer co-operated when she tried to piece her thoughts together.

EIGHT

ELIZA

Eliza still couldn't face the porridge but opted for a fried egg on toast rather than her usual muesli. Time to live dangerously she thought. She'd been awake for hours, finally succumbing to the restlessness and going for a walk in the early morning darkness. Shapes that she knew were the mountains and the unmistakeable sound of water lapping against the pier had given the eerieness a peace that she had breathed in greedily. It had been deceptively cold and she regretted not wearing her fleece. I am alive she said out loud scaring herself. She lost track of how long she stood gazing out in to the darkness but gradually the fingers of dawn had quietly and gently drawn back the curtains of the night and a new day had begun.

"Morning there." the now familiar voice said disturbing her out of her reverie

"Wasn't sure if you had any plans for today but the mini bus we've hired to take us to the race came yesterday. Anyway we've decided to pay the extra and use it for a trip to Armadale Castle this morning. Its a twelve seater and theres only eleven of us so if you wanted a lift it would be no trouble. "

Eliza looked back at the runner trying to form words but failing.

"We'll be leaving at ten" Pete continued awkwardly, unnerved at Eliza's lack of a response. "and will be back about two I expect.You can do your own thing when we get there and its only a twenty minute or so drive so if you want to come you would be more than welcome. The gardens are well worth seeing and there's a museum there. Weather's due to be good too"

Eliza had read about the castle in the information pack she had found in her room, along with a spray for the legendary Skye midges and a complimentary mini bottle of whiskey which she had been tempted to take as a christmas present. She didn't know who she would give it to though. Perhaps her boss at the library, Norman Harwood. Though he might think it an odd thing for her to give him, especially as she didn't know if he drank and she could hardly tell him that it had been a freebie. Maybe she should just leave it for the next guest. At least she would use the little sachets of coffee and shortbread biscuits she kept putting in her bag, once she was back at her bedsit.

"No need to decide now," Pete concluded "but if you fancy coming just meet us outside in the car park before ten"

He smiled and left her to her finish her egg.

She would have to make a decision now. A wave of panic swept over her and with it the familiar feeling of wanting to run away. Trying to get a grip of herself and desperately fighting the fear that had welled up inside she closed her eyes and gradually got her breathing

37

back under control. She would love to see the castle gardens but feared the thought of having to talk to the others. Of more being asked of her than she could cope with. It was just too much. She would have to say no. The invitation had spoiled her mood. She was a failure and useless and the sickly mix of depression and self pity stuck in her throat and caused her head to throb mercilessly.

She didn't have any real plans. Just another walk and more time spent watching the water and the constantly changing colours of the sky and horizon. It had been enough. Good even. Now it felt as if the colours had faded and dusk had come much too soon.

She left the restaurant, hardly noticing the seagull of which she had grown so fond. Every morning and evening, when the tide went out, the bird, came and tossed the seaweed here, there and everywhere with that fiercesome beak searcing for food. If throwing seaweed ever became an Olympic sport the gull was definitely gold medal material. She had wondered why it was always on its own. They mated for life didn't they, like swans? A lump formed in Elizas throat. Had the gull lost its partner? Why was the world filled with so much loneliness and pain?. She hated it. She hated everything. Herself. Life. Why the hell had she ever got on that train and come here.

"May see you later" As she slowly made her way back to her room. Pete's voice once again cut through her thoughts. He was becoming a nuisance.

MARCUS

Marcus liked Ellen. He liked her house. He liked her laugh. He liked her body. Most of all he liked the fact that once they had done the business she got up, showered, dressed and put East Enders on. He didn't love her and he didn't have any idea how old she was. They had got talking in the pub one night about ten years ago and he'd been going round ever since. Except of course while he'd been inside. She had been the only one to write to him there. Then only because he owed her fifty quid. He didn't pay her for sex. He hadn't sunk that low but he did help out with bills. Her hairdressers bill alone must have been something as her hair was always a different colour and a different style every time he saw her. Blond, black, blue even. She had a face he would describe as interesting rather than pretty and a body that sported three tattoos. A butterfly. A cross and of all things a balloon with the words Mum and Dad in. She could be forty five Equally she could be thirty five. He didn't really care. He'd got used to her but if she moved away he wouldn't miss her. He hadn't when he was inside and likewise he knew she wouldn't shed a tear for him if he ever moved on.

He never stayed the night and he never ate there. But she never rushed him and if she was expecting someone else later she never showed it. Occasionally he wondered about her past or who had gone round while he had been inside. Not often though. It was none of his business. Presumably something somewhere hadn't worked out. It was hard to tell. Her pale blue eyes gave nothing away and the absence of photographs and personal items in the rooms offered no clues.

He put fifty quid on the table in the hall and let himself out. It was still early but he couldn't face the pub. Perhaps he'd go to the chippy. He didn't much like the Chinese bloke who ran it, but the chips were good and he realised that he was starving. He always was after sex. He'd go mad and have fish and pickled onions. He smiled and hummed as he turned onto the High Street.

EDITH

Edith turned on her side. She couldn't sleep and yet another night was playing out frame by frame like a boring black and white film. Marcus had brought her fish and chips in when he'd come home. Enjoyed them too she had. Though they had given her indigestion. He'd not said much. Just put them down by her side with a plastic fork. He never stayed in her room long for which she was thankful. Less chance of him getting wound up if his visits were short. She'd thanked him and shortly after had heard the television go on. Unlike him to go to bed early but it was barely eleven when she heard his heavy tread on the stairs. She could hardly believe that she could have given birth to him. Six foot three and her barely five two. Maybe he was working again. She assumed he would go back to his painting and decorating. It wasn't as if he had many options. School hadn't suited him and his inability to concentrate for very long had made the lessons a form of torture for him. She could see that. These days he would be classed as having special needs. In those days he was just trouble. The mother in her felt sad. Had she helped him enough? Had she favoured Eliza so very much. It was just that Eliza was no trouble. With her head in a book and her placid temperament. Time and time again she had begged Richard to spend more time with the boy. Never happened though. Not really. Not until Marcus was fifteen and left school. Then it was too late. Richard got a gofer. Marcus got a bit of money in his pocket and another criminal was born. She wondered how many mothers were frightened of their sons. Or their daughters for that matter. Was Marcus evil? She wished the local vicar would come and visit her again. She had so many questions going around in her head. The pastoral visitor must be due again soon surely. Didn't she come each month? Or was it every two months? Straining to remember things exhausted her so much. How had it come to this? And why were the nights so long? She tried to remember the words of the anthem that had been sung at Compline in the days when she still went to church. From nowhere they formed in her mind and in a ragged voice she sang:

Before the ending of the day.
Creator of the world we pray.
That with thy wanted favour thou.
Would be our guard and keeper now.

From all ill dreams defend our eyes.
From nightly fears and fantasies.

Tread underfoot our ghostly foe.
That no pollution we may know.

O Father that we ask be done.
Through Jesus Christ thy only Son.
Who with the Holy Ghost and thee.
Doth live and reign eternally.

Tears coursed down her face.Though what the tears were trying to say, she didn't know.

NINE

Sitting in the sun in Armadale gardens.Eliza closed her eyes and listened to the birds. Did they sing for the sheer joy of being alive she wondered? If so in that second she would join them.

She hadn't at all meant to go. Once back in her room, she had slumped on the bed feeling a total failure and wishing she could evaporate like the morning mist . A knock on the door had halted her spiralling thoughts and the young couple who serviced the rooms stood there smiling.

"We can come back the girl" said in her broken English, apologetic and cheerful at the same time.

"No no it's alright" Eliza grabbed her coat and bag and left them to the room she no longer had any desire to stay in. Skye, which had been occupied since the Mesolithic period and which for a time had been ruled by the Norse only had a population of just over ten thousand people. So why couldn't she get any peace? There were only supposed to be 6.04 people per square kilometre but wherever she went people found her. She felt trapped even here where the mountains and lochs spoke the language of solitude. They lied.

It had been dreadful timing. Just as she had walked out of the hotel across the car park the group were gathering for their outing. Pete waved and came over

"So glad you decided to come" he said with such sincerity and enthusiasm it seemed easier to get on the wretched mini bus with all the wretched runners than to try and explain she just wanted to be on her own. Was that really too much to ask?

In spite of her grumpiness and doing her best not to catch the eye of any of the others, she found herself gazing out of the mini bus window with a sense of awe. The barreness of the road made it look like a desert. She wouldn't have been surprised to see camels appear in the distance. You could go mad she thought looking at that day after day. Yet it was beautiful. Not a blade of grass to be seen but still the land moved her. The conversations of the group intrigued her too. There were six other women and five men. Three couples and four on their own, although Trudy and Joe had been friends since Uni. Angie and Mike, Thomas and Abby, Sal and Iain, Lorraine, Trudy, Joe, Pete and Libby. It was the second year in a row that they had met up. Only eight of them were actually running. Three of the partners – Eliza wasn't sure who was married and who wasn't were just coming along as cheerleaders and to enjoy the island which they all seemed to love with a passion that Eliza recognised in her own heart.

To her relief, they didn't ask her anything about herself and when the mini bus drew up at the castle, they all piled out and bought their own tickets in the richly stocked gift shop. Going off into the gardens in twos and threes. Libby she noticed went off on her own as did Pete.

To give the others a head start, she had gone to the toilet first and now two hours later found herself day dreaming. Overcome again with the sense of promise and reassurance that seemed to be in the very atmosphere of this inspirational island.

The trees, carrying their leaves with effortless grace and with the essence of eternity that nature somehow exuded, had charmed and delighted her. She had wandered slowly around the gardens discovering the remains of the old stone laundry before coming to a statue of a raven that sat black and bold on a plinth outside the museum of Skye which had opened in 2002.

The castle was the spiritual home of the Macdonald clan and she had spent an absorbing hour in the museum learning something of their history and about the famous figures who had visitied. Flora MacDonald, famed for helping Bonnie Prince Charlie to flee Scotland after the Jacobites' defeat at Culloden, was married there on 6 November 1750. Samuel Johnson and James Boswell visited in 1773.She especially liked the quote:

> ."Na sloigh as feart san gcruinne A muirn a mire a bhfighnamh; Ni comhnairt bheith ' na bhfeagmhais: Ni h-eibhneas gan Chlainn Domhnall"

> "The best people in the round world, their joyousness, their keenness, their effectiveness; without them is no strength; it is no joy without Clan Donald"

Beginning to feel hungry but torn too as she was tempted to linger on the bench until they were due to leave. She could feel her energy levels dropping, so reluctantly she made her way to the restaurant. The youngest of the couples, Sal and Iain who were in their early thirties, waved at her and hesitantly she made her way to the table, where Pete, Joe and Trudy were also seated. Out of nowhere she felt a sense of pleasure. Confidence crept up, then quickly retreated as she worried about how she might contribute to the conversation. In the end words came easily as she recounted her morning. Skye spoke for itself and she spoke as though in love.

"Skye has got her" said Iain laughing. "It does that you know It gets right into your soul and hooks you."

Eliza had smiled. He was right. Skye knew her like no one ever had. The barrenness. The beauty. The mist. They understood. They understood everything. For a moment tears threatened to well up. How would she ever leave?

MARCUS

It was time to go. It was nearly twelve and he was still sitting in the cafe staring at the paper which he had long since stopped reading. Prison had changed him. Not for better or for worse, He was just different. He couldn't properly formulate his thoughts or understand his feelings. It was as if his old self was looking over his shoulder all the time. Trying to see things as they had been. Trying to convince him that nothing had changed, though everything had. Everything. His routine and his life seemed empty, his dreams childish and his longing for wealth ridiculous. He'd never be rich. Not unless he did something crazy. He toyed with the idea of selling the house. Must be worth at least a hundred and fifty grand. Social services could take care of his mother and he could go abroad, start again. Or at least he could once he had seen out the conditions of his probation. He was sick of Wellington. He was sick of the look in his mothers eyes. He was sick of everything. He had only been out three days and already fear was being to collect in the pit of his stomach. Coiled tight for now but he knew it could unleash itself without warning as anger. Anger that frightened him as much as it did others. In one sense it did a great job. Not many people would ever think to cross him. A few had tried, and had had accidents. Damage to their cars. Late night phone calls to their partners or spouses that had usually brought them back in line. In truth he was small fry. He was part of no mafia and he was no Kray twin. The threat of violence he posed gained him some grudging respect from people around him in the pub and bookies. It was enough most of the time. If charm was needed for the old folks in the houses he decorated, then he could turn that on too. Especially with the ladies. He always encouraged them to chat. He needed to know if they had family looking out them. Family who might query the prices they got for their valuables. When in a moment of weakness he had told one of the prison visitors that he liked`old` people`and their stories.The silly pratt had suggested he think about working in a care home. For crying out loud. Long hours, rubbish pay. He had played along but what a joke. It had given him the idea of offering to do some voluntary decorating in a couple of the local care homes though. Might get a chance to get his hands on some good stuff. In the end he had thought it too risky. They had CCTV cameras everywhere these days and he wasn't about to jeopardise his freedom for a few quid. Still was something to tuck up his sleeve you never know he had thought.

"Finished with that mug have you?"

The young lad who cleared the tables in the cafe asked

Marcus for a moment went to say something that would make the boy think twice about approaching his table again. In the end though he just couldn't be bothered. He picked up his paper and slammed the cafe door behind him as he left. Let everyone stare. He didn't care. At this moment in time he didn't care about anything. Perhaps he should get another dog. It had been a long time since Daffy had died. Daffy and completely dozy she'd been a reject guidedog. Mmm definite possibility. He headed for the betting shop with a renewed spring in his step.

EDITH

Her carer was quiet today,which suited her fine. It was one of those days when as she opened her eyes a massive wave of disappointment washed over her. Her first conscious thought was one of regret. She was still here. She didn't especially want to die. She just didn't want to live like this and she didn't want Marcus to be back. Part of her hoped he would reoffend and get sent back to prison, but then she immediately felt guilty. She didn't want anyone else to suffer at his hands. He had only been home three days and already her nerves were shot to pieces. To be fair to him, he hadn't given her any reason to think he would hurt her. He'd been moody and monosyllabic, but hadn't he always been? Well, maybe not always. As a little boy he had been gentle. Easily bored but a son to be proud of. She knew Richard hadn't been proud of him. Marcus knew too and it ate away at him. She had seen his face when she had broken the news of his fathers death. There had been no grief. Surprise and a fleeting look of bewilderment had crossed his features, regret even. but no grief. Mind you, she hadn't felt much either. Maybe a sense of relief. A sense of freedom. Shortlived, but there. Suddenly she felt pity for Richard. You live on this planet for more than fifty years and when you go nobody misses you. Self pity followed,would anyone miss her? Eliza loved her she knew that, but whether she would miss her, Edith wasn't so sure.

"Can I get you anything else love?"

The carers Brummie voice interrupted her thoughts.

"There's the usual sandwich there. Cheese and pickle today, a banana and yoghurt. Strawberry flavour. Be Wimbledon soon so thought we should enter into the spirit of things. That Rafa Nadal is gorgeous don't you think?"

Too irritable to say anything pleasant. Edith just smiled, which seemed to please the carer whose name she couldn't bring to mind. It was there somewhere in the mire of her brain but she was damned if she could locate it. Damned. Was she damned? She tried to go on believing and she did so love the psalms with all their cries and their battles and their triumphs. The psalmist knew what it was to be in the depths and yet somehow he kept faith She must re- read them for herself. If only the vicar would call. She would write him a note. saying that she understood how busy he was, or was it a she now? Oh for goodness sake she berated herself can't you remember anything.

The front door closed and her link with the outside world went off to see her next client. Oh Eliza, Eliza she silently cried inside. Where are you? Her cry was as empty as her days. How could Eliza possibly come and visit her now. The realisation that she might never see her daughter again was a blow too far and sobs wracked through her aged body. She might only be sixty nine but she had the frame and the mind of a woman twenty years her senior and she was ready to die. She must get in contact with the vicar. Arrange her funeral. She lay back on her pillow. That would be the days task. Choosing the hymn she would have and which psalm.

TEN

No one had seemed in a hurry to get back and so they had wandered down to the gift shops by the pier. Eliza had bought her mother a beautiful hand knitted tartan scarf. It had been an impulse purchase and now as she sat on the bed in her room and looked at it she wondered if her mother would ever go out again to wear it. She had desperately wanted to send her a postcard and try to describe the island and the mystical way it seemed to wrap its arms around her. Every moment of every day Skye was alive. Mist, clouds, sun, haze, water, always changing, always on the move. Whenever she looked out of her window the mountains in the distance drew her to themselves. Dark, brutal even by dusk, they were transfigured by sunlight and she felt as though she had always known and been known by them. The landscape was beyond her powers of description but she would have liked to share something of it with the woman she loved and worried about so much.

She didn't want Marcus to know where she was. It was as simple as that. It wasn't as if he would come to find her. He had no desire to see her again. He still blamed her for what had happened which was incomprehensible to everyone except himself. His knowing she was here would tarnish the experience. It was bad enough that he was in her thoughts and that fear of him still coursed through her body as real as her blood.

To her surprise she had enjoyed the day out. Libby had bought everyone an ice cream and they had all stood leaning against the harbour wall gazing out across the water. The silence had been perfect. Only the gulls above their heads had felt the need to talk. Almost as one they had turned away and walked back to the mini bus, each filled with their own thoughts and dreams. Skye made a child of you Eliza thought. It made you wonder and play and believe in magic. She hadn't gone over for supper. She was too tired, but happy tired. Being amongst people had always sapped her of energy. Beneath the surface she was never able to quite relax and the tension exhausted her. She also didn't want to leave the new place inside herself that Skye had guided her to. It felt safe. The landscape was cocooning her from her past and the desperate memories she carried around like dead weights. Yet at the same time it was releasing her to be a woman again. To take off her grave clothes as it were and put on life. As the final threads of daylight gave way to the darkness of a velvet sky,she ran a bath and lay back as content as she could ever be. Even the scars on her body seemed paler. Could she grow to love her body again? Best not to think about it too much. One moment at a time. The thought that she only had three days left of her holiday cut through her like a knife She wanted to stay longer. More than she had ever wanted anything in the world. She wanted to stay on Skye forever.

MARCUS

For the first time since he had been back. Marcus had
lost at the bookies. Only eighty quid but it was enough
to put him in a filthy mood. Made worse by the fact that
the horse he had given to three old guys who looked to
him for a tip had romped home at four to one and they
had all won twenty quid each. Tobacco money for the
week one of them had said as he collected his winnings.
It was all Marcus could do to stop himself putting his
fist in the smug old git's face. His counsellor had once
asked him how it was that the same hands that could
gently stroke an animal could be smashed into another
mans body without a second thought. Marcus hadn't
been able to answer and as he walked further away
from Wellington on the Taunton road he had tried to
remember when he had first been violent. The noise of
the cars racing past him and the heat of the day took
their toll and he gave up thinking and when he got as far
as the garden centre he went in and bought a tea and
pastry. He would need to watch himself. He was eating
far too much. Sitting in cafes watching the world go by
was a losers game. Like bloody gambling. Still, he had
a job lined up, starting Monday. Dec had a client who
wanted her bathroom and front room spruced up before
she put her house up for sale. She had the beginnings
of dementia and that coupled with loneliness since the
loss of her husband had led her to make the decision
to move into an Abbeyfield home. She could look after
herself but had told Marcus when he had gone round
to give her a quote, that she was being sensible. She

53

didn't have children, they had lost their only daughter, Natalie to leukaemia when she was eleven so she had to look out for herself. Her husband Eric had left her well provided for so she couldn't complain.

Neither could Marcus. He was on to a winner there. She had told him that she would be away Tuesday and Wednesday on a Mothers Union trip to Cornwall but he was to let himself in and help himself to tea or coffee or whatever he wanted. Well he would certainly do that. She even thanked him for coming. It was pathetic the way they were always so grateful.

It is such a relief to have found someone I can trust she had said as he had left. That nice man at the estate agent said you were the best and that I wasn't to worry. Not for a moment had Marcus felt guilty. She had more than she needed and she would only leave the rest to the church or some other lost cause. No, he and Mrs Wilkinson were going to get on just fine.

EDITH

It was Friday. Desert Island Discs was on the radio so it had to be. Some musician called Wakeman. She hadn't heard of him but liked the Kenny Ball and the Jazzmen track he had picked. If she was right and she was almost certain that she was.It meant her carer would be bringing new library books. It was the highlight of the week wondering what books she would be given. It had been Debbie Macomber last week with her tales from a friendly knitting shop. The week before it had been. Oh bother, she couldn't remember. No matter she was sure she had enjoyed it at the time.

"Hi Edith how you doing?"

The carer she liked the most, Lara, swept into her room, a book under her arm and a tray in her hands. Edith hauled herself upright and after her daily wash looked to see what treasure Lara had brought. She was interested in the book more than the food. She ate because she had to, she read because she wanted to. No prizes for guessing where Eliza got her love of words from. Food like the tablets she took kept her alive. Books kept her sane. At least she thought they did and if they didn't they at least made madness bearable.

"Got you something a bit different this week" Lara said pleased with herself. "It's set in Venice and called Miss Garnet's Angel. It's by a woman called Sally Vickers. Anyway it was being handed back in just as I walked past the desk and the lady was raving about it so I grabbed it for you. Brought you a Belgian bun to go with it, thought you could go all European today." She smiled.

Edith smiled back. Lara was the youngest of the three carers who took it in turns to help her. She was barely twenty yet she was as thoughtful as a daughter might be. Fun too with her pierced eye brows and bottle red hair. She was a one off. Complete opposite of her real daughter who would never even wear a red jumper let alone dye her hair. Sensible you could describe Eliza's dress sense. Flat shoes,full length skirts. Plain blouses and jumpers. You would never be able to guess what season it is was by Eliza's clothes. Edith suddenly felt sorry for her daughter. She had missed out. She had never been young, In years yes, but in spirit never. She hadn't travelled.Never gone to parties or raves or whatever it was that kids went to. She realised with horror that as a mother she had been selfish. She hadn't encouraged Eliza enough. She had been glad, even manipulated her into staying in with her. Or going out with her to the pictures. Even bingo once or twice. No wonder she had never met anyone or even made any real friends. It was her fault. Everything was all her fault. She screamed inside with a bitterness as vicious as her son. As Lara called out goodbye, the walls began to close in on her and the terror of what had happened unleashed itself again. I'm sorry Eliza. I'm so sorry she howled as tears wracked her body until she barely had the strength to breathe.

ELEVEN

ELIZA

Eliza had just put her book down ready to turn off the light when a note was pushed under her door. It was from Pete reminding her that the mini bus would be leaving for Portree for the Half Marathon at 7.45 in the morning.The hotel had agreed to do an early buffet breakfast for the runners which would be available from seven.No pressure it said.

Portree was the capital of Skye so it would be good to have a look round Eliza thought. It was situated on the east side of the island overlooking a sheltered bay, and surrounded by hills. Ben Tianavaig to the south, Suidh Fhinn or Fingal's Seat to the west, and Ben Chrachaig, to the north. Further north along the road to Staffin was the famous Old Man of Storr. Across the bay to the east, the Island of Raasay could be seen with its distinctive conical hill, Dun Caan.

Portree was only about 200 years old and was created as a fishing village at the beginning of the 19th century by the then Lord MacDonald. The name Portree or Port Righ, King's Port in Gaelic, was popularly thought to derive from a visit by King James V of Scotland in 1540 but the area around the harbour was called Portree or Portray long before the arrival of the king. Its name really came from the Gaelic for Port on the Slope.

It was less than forty miles away but would take over an hour to get to. She told herself she had survived the conversations earlier so why shouldn't she give it a go? She would see how she felt in the morning. She usually managed to talk herself out of doing anything vaguely exciting or adventurous. Always too many things that might or might not happen. Too many expectations she might not be able to fulfill. In the end she would end up so exhausted thinking about it all she gave up and stayed in. How she wished she could be gung ho, say yes to anything and worry about it afterwards. She had been reading about a local hero, a mountaineer called John Mackenzie. Born in 1856 he started climbing at the age of six and in 1906 had made the first ascent of Sgurr Mhic Choinnich naming it the Cloch. Now known as the inaccessible pinnacle and yet he had tackled it and gone on to be the first professional mountain guide to work in Britain. Why couldn't she be brave like that? Instead of being Ms. Boring, Careful and Anxious. Sleep would never come now. She made herself a cup of tea and sat in the darkness looking out across the water. She couldn't see anything except the blackness of night. There were a few lights still on in a couple of rooms in the hotel cottages to the left of the bay. It was now gone midnight and she wondered what they were thinking about. Though she couldn't see the mountains, she knew they were there. They weren't afraid. They stood strong and bold, confident in their ability to withstand anything the Scottish climate or humankind could throw at them. They had stood for thousands of years and would be standing for thousands of years to come. She thought of Pete approaching seventy and yet ready to tackle a race that many half his age would shrink away from. She couldn't even run a hundred metres. Her thoughts turned to her mother. The same age as Pete and yet all but confined to her bed. Guilt made her close the curtains and as she washed her tea cup. She wondered whether she would ever see her mother again. She couldn't visit now Marcus was back. Why hadn't she gone to see her before coming to Skye? It had been March, Mothers Day the last time she had made the trip back to Wellington and the house that had been both home and hell. To celebrate his seventieth birthday Pete had said he was going to run the Edinburgh Marathon next May. What would her mother do on her seventieth? Would she even know it was her birthday? Questions, guilt and the pain she recognised so well battled for room in her brain until she heard the first sounds of morning outside. She supposed she must have slept but exhaustion was all she felt as she headed to the bathroom. It was only six thirty. She had another half an hour to agonise about whether to go to Portree or not. Maybe she would just go back to bed.

MARCUS

Marcus had had a thought. A rather good one as it happened. He would clear out Eliza's room and make it into a guest room. It wouldn't cost much, he could do the work himself. Then he could rent it out and make a bit more a month. Get a chap in who didn't mind basic and he would be quids in. It wasn't as if Eliza would ever come back. She would never set foot in the house again so why pretend she would. Anyway it was his house and he would do what he wanted with It. Which included leaving it to the RSPCA. He had scribbled out a note to that intent and would get it all done legally when he next had a bit of spare cash. It wasn't as if he would be kicking the bucket anytime soon, He grinned, imagining the look on everyones face when they found out. SURPRISE SURPRISE! God forbid that he should go first though. He was the youngest after all. No Eliza would never come back and he had no desire to set eyes again on the woman who had cost him over seven years of his life. She had quite simply led him on. It might not have been quite right, her being his half sister and all that. But she had been the one up for it. She had encouraged and teased him then called it rape, the bitch.He snarled inside at the very thought of her. Played the innocent butter wouldn't melt in her mouth victim. Everyone believed her too which still enraged him. He was the victim, not her. He was the one who had been cooped up, whose name had been dragged through the mud. It was always the bloke who got done and it made him sick.

Consumed by the thought that the world owed him, and knowing he had unfinished business to sort out later. Marcus turned off the light and lay in the dark, listening to the sounds in the street outside. It was never quiet. Just like prison. Always someone somewhere making a noise or kicking off. The world was full of whingers, just like his mother. She might never say anything outright, but she punished him with her silence. The way she looked at him, or rather the way she avoided looking at him exuded disgust and disapproval. He shouldn't have hurt her of course he shouldn't. It was her who went for him with the bread knife though wasn't it. She was the one who poked her nose in trying protect her precious Eliza. It had been none of her business. Eliza had it coming to her. It been an accident her getting cut so bad it really had and if no one believed him then they could all go to hell. He was out. He was back and he would do what he wanted, when he wanted. Sod the rest of the world.

EDITH

Sleep again eluded Edith, so she flicked on the bedside lamp and picked up the library book. Miss Garnet was a revelation and she only turned the light off when she could no longer focus on the page or keep her eyes open. She remembered the film The Bucket List with that crazy actor, what was he called Jack something…. Jack Nicholson that was it and that rather nice man Morgan Freeman. For some reason the final words from the film came to her Jack Nicholson had said of Freemans character, he died with his eyes closed but his heart open. The speech had moved her at the time and it did again now. That was how she wanted to die. With her heart open. The only trouble with that was that her heart was sealed up, stony and dour. Fear, regret, bitterness. She had harboured them all in her pitiful heart until love and trust and hope had dried up. She could forgive Marcus for

61

what he had done to her. She knew he hadn't planned to injure her so badly. She could never, not in a million years though, forgive him for what he had done to Eliza. It had been sheer viciousness and he had never shown an ounce of remorse. Not that she could see anyway. Presumably he had spun the prison governor a load of lies or else he would still be locked up. She should have seen it coming but it had never once entered her head that he was capable of such evil Because that's what it was evil. Her own son, raping his own flesh and blood. You read about things like that in the paper of course you did. It didn't happen to people like them though did it. The only mercy was the fact that Eliza hadn't fallen pregnant. It had destroyed her though. She had shrunk before her eyes, getting thinner and thinner. Withdrawing more and more until finally she had been sectioned. It had saved her life but it hadn't healed her. Perhaps nothing, or no one ever would be able to do that. Edith sighed, aware that her thoughts were spiralling down again. If only sleep would come, and come soon.

TWELVE

ELIZA

It was just no good. Eliza would never be be able to stomach porridge again. The runners were tucking in with slices of banana and honey heaped on top. She stuck to muesli and toast as ever. Going to the race had seemed the only way to escape the relentless attack of negativity in her head. She had made an effort and worn the one and only pair of trainers she possessed. It hadn't made her fit in any better though. She felt old and tatty in her cords and baggy jumper, from another age. Now just stop it she told herself sternly. No one cares what you look like or what you wear so get on with it.

Pete had been right about the atmosphere, but wrong about the weather. There was a wonderful buzz at Portree School where the race would start and finish. A chilly wind was the only unwelcome guest at the gathering. There had been a quiet excitement on the journey there. Pre race nerves and times, splits she thought they called them, that had to be hit each mile to achieve a PB which she discovered was a personal best. Talk of training and medals petered out and each soon settled into the silence, taking in the incredible landscape once again.

One part of the journey had terrified her and she had had to look away as there seemed to be very little between the bus, the side of the road and a very long drop. Already she was dreading that bit of the journey coming back. If anyone noticed her fear they didn't say and eventually the road levelled out and they made the descent into Portree.

There must have been seven hundred runners milling around. Some doing strenuous warmups, others sitting on the grass. All Elizas pre conceived ideas of what a runner looked like went out of the window. Every shape and size of person was represented. Some had athletic club vests on and shorts and looked like Scottish versions of Mo Farah. Others were in leggings, tracksuits, long sleeved tops of every colour. Dozens of charities were represented, There were a few kilts and even a chap in a Superman costume. It was wonderful, she completely forgot everything as she was swept up in the camaraderie. Many were running the race for the second or third time. Friendships were renewed, jokes shared, hopes outlined. For some it was obviously a very serious business, but for most it seemed like a great day out. Though why anyone would choose to run thirteen miles on their day off she couldn't fathom. She was jealous though. She wanted to be with them on the start line. She wanted to be one of them. Could she really set herself the goal of coming back next year to run? No that was ridiculous. She was getting carried away.

Pete had told her that the Skye Half Marathon had first been run in 1984 over the distance of thirteen point eight miles with 140 runners braving the undulating course. It had been part of a week of events celebrating the riches of Skye and had grown year on year. The first winner had somehow managed to finish in a mind blowing one hour and sixteen minutes. It had become one of the most popular races in the Scottish calendar and attracted competitors from as far away as America. Mostly though it was a gathering of Scots celebrating their heritage and pitting themselves against the landscape of this incredible island. She had even heard bagpipers mentioned though she couldn't see any. The course was a single loop with a steady climb from the eight to the eleven mile mark before the road dropped back down again returning to the Fingal Centre where they started. She had thought it would be a long wait for the finishers to stagger in so she had brought her book. However some would be crossing the finish line in just over an hour and a half. Unbelieveable. Pete had hoped to finish in around 2 hours forty. Libby in three hours, it was her first long race and the hopes of the others lay somewhere in between. Only Thomas was expecting to break two hours.

The four of them who were weren't running squeezed themselves in at the front of the crowd and clapped and cheered as the race started. It was a colourful blur of smiling faces and bright vests and as each of their group passed by the four cheerleaders shouted their names proudly and with great excitement. Secretly wishing they were out there running too. Once they were all underway, Eliza made her way to the refreshment stall for a much needed hot chocolate. Being happy was thirsty work she smiled to herself as she settled down with Rachel Joyce's

Unlikely Pilgrimage of Harold Fry, in a world of her own. A world that for once she was actually glad to be in.

MARCUS

In the end Marcus hadn't trashed the pub. He'd been more subtle and torched it. His mother gave him an alibi:

No officer. I didn't go out all evening. You can check with my mother. I watched the television and had an early night. Reformed character me, as you know he had smirked. What a shame. Such a nice landlord too. Actually the fire had hardly got going before the alarm was raised so there was minimal damage. Neat really. A bit of re decorating to cover the smoke damage, but the pub was still open. He would go in on Sunday, bold as brass. He was back alright. Oh yes he was back. They would never be able to prove it was him. They knew though. They knew alright. He wouldn't be taking too many risks. Not worth it. There were times though when people needed to be taught a lesson. No one was disrespectful to Marcus Grady. No one.

EDITH

The police came this morning. I thought I was dreaming she told the carer. Or more like it having another nightmare. It was real enough though. Terribly nice young man and a police woman too.

"We are really sorry to intrude Mrs Grady but there was an incident last night the young officer began, in the Golden Cockerel. We don't for one minute suspect that Marcus was involved."

What a good liar Edith thought, his blue eyes never stopped looking at her and his voice never quavered.

"However," the officer continued. "We are checking the whereabouts of everyone who is a regular there and of course your Marcus' name came up."

'Your Marcus' Edith had shuddered when the officer had said those words. She had wanted to scream out He's not my Marcus. He's my cross. He's my punishment for marrying a man I didn't love. She tried to concentrate as the officer continued. What did he say his name was Fisher was it? Oh Lord she was going to pieces. The gangly and earnest young man barely looked out of his teens. Though he was probably nearer thirty than twenty. Everyone looked younger than they were these days . Except her.

"Your son,when we interviewed him, said that he was home all last night, watching the television and that you would be able to verify that. He said he hadn't gone out at all and had gone to bed about eleven."

It was true the television had been on. She had heard the front door open and close though. While the local news was on so would have been after ten thirty. He had had the sound up much louder than usual. Now she knew why. He'd wanted her to hear it and to remember that it had been going all evening.

There was an uncomfortable silence and the officer said. "We are truly sorry to have had to come and

67

disturb you, but if you could just confirm that your son was in all night we can go on our way and leave you in peace."

Leave her in peace. Didn't they understand that she would never be at peace? Not until she was in her grave. Again the urge to scream rose up from within her but she found herself saying

"Yes, he was in all night." It was a lie but inspite of a desperate longing to shout he went out, he went out, so send him back to prison NOW NOW NOW she stuck to her story.

"Are you absolutely sure Mrs Grady" the police woman was speaking for the first time since they had come into her room. "I know he's your son and it is hard not to cover up for them sometimes. Family ties go deep we understand that. However we are treating this as a very serious incident and whilst we don't want you to think we are picking on your son because he has been in trouble in the past, we do want to get to the truth. You needn't be afraid of telling the truth" she said more softly. "If Marcus did go out and was involved in the fire, it would be a violation of his parole and he would be sent back to prison. Now I'm not suggesting you would want that but just so that you know. Now take your time before you answer. Are you absolutely sure that Marcus didn't go out at all last night. That he was here all evening watching television?"

"Yes" she said in a weak voice "I'm sure."

There was little more the two police oficers could do. They thanked her for her time, apologised again for disturbing her and left.

Marcus showed them out and then came up to her room with a mug of tea and the paper which she noticed was yesterdays.

"I don't why they thought it was me" he said. "Thanks for putting them right. Drink your tea while it's hot and I'll see you later." He closed the door which she wished he wouldn't do and ten minutes later he was gone. Leaving Edith to the silence which that morning sounded thunderous.

You might have sent him back to prison she said to no one. He would get out again though wouldn't he. Wouldn't he. If I was still alive them what do you think he would have done to me Eh Eh?

Afraid of him? Of course she was bloodywell afraid of him. She was the one in prison. Couldn't they see that? She was the one confined behind the bars of disability, guilt and fear. Why couldn't she just die and be done with it. He would offend again. The police would come back. It was an endless nightmare. As long as Marcus lived and breathed she would never have a moment when she wasn't on edge. Eliza was best out of it. The thought of her daughter brought the tears she had been holding back all morning. Cold tea and yesterdays news sat on the bed side cabinet looking dispassionately on.

THIRTEEN

ELIZA

"Go on Pete. Go on you can do it. Keep going. Not far now. YEESSSS!!". Eliza's sense of joy and pride as a grey haired man she barely knew crossed the line knew no bounds and when he made his way over to the group with his medal around his neck clutching his goody bag she couldn't help but give him a hug just as the others did. His blue top and white shorts were dripping with sweat and he looked as if he might collapse any minute. The give away though was a gleam in his eye and she knew she was looking at a happy man. They would have to wait for their official times but he had stopped his watch at 2 hours 27 minutes and fourteen seconds. Forty three seconds faster than last year. Thomas had run one hour forty one and Libby was their only runner left to complete.

Eliza couldn't believe how fast the time had gone. She had barely read a chapter when crowds started gathering at the finish line and she had watched the first and fastest runners sprint in as if they had merely done a jog around the block. As the time went on, the runners looked more and more weary though most managed to bravely put on a final sprint. Libby in her pink top and pink leggings did her best too to increase speed at the end but the effort had taken its toll. Bloody hills she said with what little breath she had left. She said it smiling though she had finished in two hours fifty nine minutes and fifty three seconds. Breaking three hours was a thrilling achievement and everyone high fived her. She was as much a hero as the first runner across the line in a stunning one hour and thirty two minutes. Libby was by no means the last runner home and it was a proud bunch who went into Portree itself for a celebratory meal at a quirky little place called Cafe Arriba. It was only a two minute walk from the main square where Pete had parked the mini bus and had super views across the quay. It was painted in the brightest colours imaginable and nothing matched. The food though was delicious and as Eliza looked around the table at her eleven companions, different as they all were, in that moment they belonged together. Tomorrow they would go their separate ways. Mike and Angie would collect their two boys from Angies sister. Sal and Iain would call in on his mother in Inverness before travelling back to Glasgow. Twelve people with twelve different lives. Some interwined. Some individual and only briefly connected by the Half Marathon. She had hardly spoken two words to most of them but somehow she cared about them. More to the point and it was a shock to realise it, she would miss the safety they gave her. After all the worries. All the fearing she wouldn't cope had disappeared like the morning mist over the mountains. They had made her stronger. At least she thought they had.The sense of dread at having to leave and return to Gloucester on Monday still hung heavy. She wouldn't think about that now. No she would enjoy the moment. She caught Pete's eye. What a dear man he was. A man she would truly like to be able to call friend.

MARCUS

Marcus had got his beloved bike out. One of the first things he had done when he got home was to check in the garage to make sure no one had nicked it. He had given it a polish, emptied the helmet of dead spiders and dust and set out for Weston Super Mere. He fancied fish and chips on the pier and he had never lost his love of amusement arcades. It would do him good. With hindsight he had been crazy to set fire to the pub. If he let pricks like Billy, the landlord wind him up he would end up back inside in no time. They just weren't worth it. He knew his mother would always vouch for him even if she didn't know what day it was half the time. He would need to use his brain though and think things through more. He had some notes in his bag from the anger management course he'd done in prison. Maybe he would take a look when he got back. Musn't throw it all away for some worthless piece of shit .

He would be starting work on Mrs Wilkinsons house on Monday so Marcus the charmer would need to be in residence. It wasn't all an act though. He did like make people feeling good about theselves. At his best he knew he did notice things and picked up how people were feeling. He could actually be quite sensitive. Though nobody would believe it, deep inside there was another

Marcus he could have been. Too late now. A memory of one winter came back to him. It had been brutal and Mrs Hibbs from three doors down had fallen and broken her hip. Without being asked, he had taken on the responsibility of walking her corgi, Beau. He was all of about eight and refused to take any money. His father had been furious and said he could have made a packet but Marcus had felt good about helping her.

Out of the way you Tosser he snarled as a young lad ran out in front of him as he came up to a crossing.

It was definitely too late now.

EDITH

Edith heard the bike start up. She had thought about selling it in spite. Would have served him right. It would have really hurt him to come home and find it gone and some days she so desperately wanted to hurt him like he had hurt her and Eliza. In the end though she had been afraid. The same recurring theme of fear fear fear. That bike, a 1980 Harley Davidson Chopper had been Richards pride and joy. Goodness knows how he had afforded it as apparently they didn't come cheap. He probably swindled it out of some poor soul she thought. Still if Marcus had gone out on it he wouldn't be home any time soon. She relaxed a bit and managed to get herself into the chair. She would finish the Sally Vickers book and see what Miss Garnet got up to. She had a feeling it would end in sadness. Though maybe death wasn't always sad. Maybe it could come as a friend. Some days she longed for it to call on her and guide her gently to a place where her mind never struggled to remember things. Where her body never ached and where she wasn't filled with a despairing exhaustion that made her feel a hundred years old. Did she want to actually die though? She didn't know. She just wanted to be at peace that was all. It wasn't too much to ask was it? The carer came late on a Saturday which she didn't mind. It was Saturday wasn't it? The mist of uncertainty slowly descended again and she hung on to the book as though for dear life. Venice, angels, Tobit, Miss Garnet was lucky, even if she did die at the end of the novel. Or maybe especially if she did.

FOURTEEN

ELIZA

"Is it my imagination Pete or are you limping?"

Pete smiled ruefully.

"Blisters! My own fault. I ran in a new pair of socks. Thought they looked the same as my usual ones but the material was slightly thicker. Hence the hobble! Never mind"

"I'm just in awe of you, war wounds and all" Eliza blurted out. "There was such a chilly wind and the route was hard and well you were all amazing."

They had arrived for breakfast at the restaurant at the same time and their conversation led them naturally to head to the same table. Eliza didn't even think about it until they were seated.

"In your honour I won't have porridge" Pete said and ordered the full works, egg, bacon, the lot. Eliza too ordered an egg and mushrooms. Which after four years of anorexia was a bigger step than Pete could know. She still feared food and was even now only beginning to rediscover what proper eating was. Portion sizes worried her and a plate full of food could still send her into a panic. This morning though, her appetite, like her confidence was in good shape.

"I'm off this afternoon" Pete said as they finished their coffees. They had chatted easily over their meal and as she had told him she was going tomorrow a huge lump formed in her throat.

Pete either didn't notice or was too polite to stare but he went quiet for a moment. Then said " I don't know if you would be interested but Libby, Thomas and I are going to sign up to run the Edinburgh Marathon next year. It's the last weekend of May. It's a bank holiday actually. We are going to stay at a retreat house for a few days, explore the city a bit after the race and then make our way up to Skye where the others will join us as usual.

It's a way off so you've got plenty of time to save and plan for the trip."

Eliza winced."Sorry that was clumsy. What I meant was that for many a visit to Skye is a one off trip of a lifetime. The answer to a call almost. The mountains are evangelists drawing folks to themselves and showing them the vastness that even they are lost in. Coming to Skye isn't cheap I know and the trip next year will be nearly two and a half weeks long It's hard to get that much time off work, Anyway to cut this rather longwinded rambling story short. I would need to know by the beginning of July so that I can book everywhere but wouldn't need any money until November time. The balance would be payable next April. I don't know your circumstances but didn't want to take it for granted you could afford it. Money's tight these days for a lot of people and it would be a fair amount.

"It's alright for me now I'm retired and my time is my own. I'm fortunate too to have a decent pension and have picked up the Scottish habit of looking after my pennies!"

Eliza was quiet. Trying to hold all the thoughts in her head.

"It would be lovely if you could join us" Pete said almost wistfully. "We have all so enjoyed your company. Even if you can't make Edinburgh, same place same time next year is our parting quip to each other and we would be glad to see you again. It's not the most original farewell but it is heartfelt." Emotions were surging through Eliza overwhelmed by the thought that they would include her. Pete smiled. "Sorry, I'm waffling put it down to post race blues."

Finally Eliza found her voice.

"I don't really know what my plans are for next year. I can't usually think more than a few days ahead. It was really out of character for me to book this trip. You were right about it being a kind of pilgrimage though. The thing is and she had to stop for a moment as she couldn't talk without her voice trembling. The thing is I don't want to leave. I feel as if I will be leaving part of me behind. The part that is alive. The part that is really me. I can't explain it and you will probably think me mad. Actually I probably am mad, but I know the landscape understands me. The mountains, the water, the birds, they know. They are so much bigger than fear and anxiety and even life itself. They just are. She blushed. It's like heaven here. Even the barrenness is beautiful. It's brutal as well. I feel that. It's harsh and winters must be as desperate as anything. Somehow though in spite of everything. In spite of all the strength the island needs to survive everything the weather can throw at it. It still has enough strength left to share. The sun, the rain, the mist even they," she paused, "even they share their glimpses of eternity with us. I just don't know how I am going to manage without them. It is simply the most inspiring place on earth." She stopped suddenly aware of how much she had said.

Pete handed her a card with his email address and mobile number on.

Eliza took it and hung her head.

"The thing is I would love to come back year. I would love to run the race with you all."

Pete smiled and raised his hand and high fived her "YES !"

"I thought you would laugh"

"Why would I do that ?

"You saw for yourself all the different runners there yesterday. There were some athletes of course there were. There were a lot of runners though for whom running is a healing process. A challenge. A way of reminding themselves that they are still alive and still capable of achieving something amazing. There were some brave brave people on that starting line yesterday. People who have overcome incredible setbacks and tragedies. You would be in very special company and well I have a sneaking suspicion that if you set your mind to it you could do anything. If you go on line there is a training programme called 'From couch to 5k' that gets your body used to running. Lots of walking to start with. There is bound to be a Park run near you. Thats a weekly timed 5k run. They're completely free and you will see people of all ages from 6 year olds to ninety year olds walking and running on their own and together. You can build up from there, then try a 10k before you tackle a half marathon.

You can always send me an email if you want any encouragement or advice. I'm no expert but I started from scratch too. Next year they are changing the route and we will be running the course in reverse. So it is a steep climb first and then downhill all the way he laughed. You are slight and have the perfect build. Go for it girl!"

It had been a long time since Eliza had been called a girl but Pete's enthusiasm wrapped itself around her fledgling hopes and for a moment she felt invincible.

The restaurant was filling up and gradually the runners and their partners all appeared. Most like Pete were leaving that day. Only Thomas and Angie were staying the extra night.

"More coffee?"

The young waitress asked and filled their cups before they had time to reply. Eliza reached for another slice of toast and Pete suddenly said

"I started running when my wife died."

"Oh Pete I'm sorry" Eliza said and meant it.

"No it's Ok. It was a long time ago. Nearly twenty years. I miss her though. As much now as in the early days. It's just not as raw now. I've grown used to it I suppose. If you ever can.

Week days weren't too bad. Though coming home to an empty house was bleak. It was the weekends that I grew to dread. I tried pottering in the garden, but my heart wasn't in it. That was Barbs domain. She loved her garden and kept it so beautifully. She would have torn me off a strip for letting it go downhill. I just couldn't summon the energy.

We couldn't have children. So there wasn't really anyone else who needed me once she had gone. It was my fault the children bit. Firing blanks the comedians call it don't they? Only it wasn't funny. I know it hurt Barb not to be a mother but she never blamed me not even when we rowed. We thought about adopting and although we felt selfish we never did get round to filling in the forms. Truth was we were happy together just the two of us and the years went by and we stopped talking about it."

"What happened?" Eliza asked when Pete went quiet

"She was diagnosed with pancreatic cancer three days after her fiftieth birthday and she didn't see fifty one. It was tough at the end and she suffered more than she ever let on I know she did. She was brave. Really brave and that as much as anything broke me."

Eliza found herself welling up at the thought of this gentle man going through so much.

"We honeymooned on Skye"

"Oh I'm sorry" Eliza butted in. "There was me talking about the island as if it was mine."

"You do apologise a lot Eliza. Do you know that?"

He sounded half joking, half serious.

Eliza blushed "I won't say I'm sorry but yes I suppose I do. It has become a habit I expect."

"That's the magic of Skye " He gazed beyond Eliza and out of the window. "It makes everyone believe it belongs to them and them alone. The mountains draw you in as though you were the first. The waters whisper only your name. They bewitch you but they never deceive. They draw out the depths of your soul and surprise you with marvellous light and possibility where you expect to see failure and darkness.

Those ten days were the happiest of my life. We were in love with one another and we were in love with this place. We walked and sat and watched and listened and laughed. The world belonged to us and to us alone! He smiled as though transported back to that time.

We had hoped to come back before Barb got too ill. There was never a right time though. Hospital appointments and treatments just took over. We seemed to spend our lives waiting. Waiting for appointments. Waiting for results. Then it was too late. She was too weak to travel. She died in the June. Was her anniversary last Wednesday actually.

Anyway while I was out in the garden each sunday trying to will myself to live. I noticed a couple of guys running past about the same time each week. In my arrogance I thought I looked younger and fitter than them so if they could do it so could I. Nearly killed me at first. Gradually though I got fitter and fitter and could run further and further. Then I started entering races. I can still remember the pride I felt when I got my first medal for completing a 10k It wasn't until I got home that it really hit me that I was alone. That Barb was gone really gone and I would never hear her voice again. That was the first time I cried. I thought I would never be able to stop. I hung the medal around our wedding photograph which probably seems a bit of a sad thing to do. It is still my favourite of all my medals though, followed closely by my one for my first Skye half marathon. A lot of runners mock the medals and goodie bags. They shouldn't though. They might just be bits of metal but they carry whole lives within them.

Slowly running became the main focus of my life. When I retired a few years ago I started volunteering with the local running group.I have met some great people and when I run I talk to Barb. So you see I am totally bonkers. "

Eliza couldn't find words and didn't want to break the flow of Pete's.

"Barb loved animals and was always sponsoring creatures all over the world. So I ran a few races for the charities she supported. Helped me not to feel so useless and surplus to requirements. Instead of a retirement party I got everyone to do a Park run with me. You can picture it can't you a whole office full of unfit and unimpressed accountants and secretaries cursing me with their every breath. Actually, they all enjoyed it, afterwards at least. A couple of them kept it up and one girl takes her children with her each week which is brilliant. "

Pete stopped suddenly as if he felt he had said too much "Sorry" he said and lowered his eyes. "Got a bit carried away. Haven't talked about Barb for a while."

"Now you are apologising." Eliza said and they both laughed.

"Seriously though," she went on." I think you are amazing. I mean really amazing."

"I have a sneaking suspicion you might be too" Pete said and she could see that he was slightly embarrased at her praise but harbouring pride too which told on his face.

Eliza fiddled with her napkin. "No I'm not" she said. "Not at all."

"I won't pry" said Pete and she knew he sensed her sadness that had suddenly enveloped the table. "Just so you know though. I don't share my life story with everyone. So thank you for listening and for coming to the race. I couldn't believe it when I heard you screaming my name. It was brilliant. Just brilliant."

Ease restored, he stood up and held out his hand which Eliza shook. "Maybe see you next year then" he grinned. "Look after yourself. You are more special than you know."

By now tears were really on a mission to escape but Eliza did her best to smile. "Thank you for everything" she said.

"Don't forget Couch to 5k" and turned and headed over to the other tables to say his goodbyes. Eliza watched as he left the restaurant and went back out into the car park blending in with the landscape she loved so much that it hurt.

She gave him ten minutes then she too said goodbye to the others and went out and down to the waters edge and sat in her favourite spot in the cove. The seagull was there tossing seaweed here, there and everywhere in a corner where the tide had gone out. Another friend she would be sorry to leave. She had kept people at arms length for so long and yet in the space of four days she had met the dearest man whom she had grown so fond of and a regal bird who shared her dreams and understood her. At least she thought he did. He was always on his own and he always seemed to spot her. A few drops of rain started to fall and the mist had insidiously crept in and blanketed the mountains in its darkness.

She picked out her notebook from her pocket and wrote

TEARS

I longed for a song.
For music to soothe my soul.
But Davids lyre was silent.
Only the sound of the wind in the trees played
and the rain falling to earth.
Drops becoming puddles.

Only the sound of the oncoming darkness remained.
A symphony of sadness, a whispering of arias.
I wept.

And tears were the words of the song
I longed for.

MARCUS

With a Mr Whippy ice cream, complete with flake in one hand and his money for the slot machines in the other, Marcus felt like a kid again.The jackpot was only a tenner but it felt great to have nothing on his mind and to be in the moment. His counsellor would be proud of him! He realised now that he had been happy as a child. You took stuff for granted when you were a kid. His dad might not have been the best but apart from the odd occasion when Marcus probably deserved it, he didn't take the belt to him too often. He put him down a lot and sneered at his love for his pet rabbits, but all in all it wasn't too bad. Mostly his dad had left him alone. Until he had grown old enough to nick things for him anyway. To be fair his mum and Eliza ran round after him making sure he was ok and covering for him when his dad was in a bad mood. For a moment he longed for those days again. The freedom of throwing off his school uniform and going out to kick a ball around. Feeding his rabbits and cycling down to the allotments to see Fred Rimmer and collect any spare greens he had. Fred used to take off his cap and scratch his bald head. Reckon I can find something for those rabbits of yours he would say. Then he'd look at Marcus and ask how he was doing. World can be a rough and unforgiving place lad he'd say so you work hard at school. You've got it in you to make something of yourself. Marcus regretted not paying more attention to Fred's wisdom. He wished too he'd gone to his funeral. Died one Sunday afternoon. Gone home for tea after a day on his patch and had a massive heart attack on the way upstairs. Marcus had read about it in the paper. To be honest he grieved more for him than he did for his own father. Fred had that way of making you believe in yourself. His dad didn't believe in anything. Certainly not in the God the minister at the crem committed his body to.

Marcus was three pounds up so he pocketed the money, picked up his helmet and wandered out of the arcade onto the pier. He watched families playing on the beach. Siblings burying each other in sand. Not that Weston was renowned for its sandy beach! Blokes in ridiculously bright Bermuda shorts throwing frisbees. Girls laughing and screaming as they ran in and out of the water. Dogs too though on their leads hurtled out as far as they could drinking the waves as they went. Then shaking themselves dry all over their owners. Boys ran after the seagulls whenever they tried to land. Thrilled when they made the birds take off again. What went on when they got home Marcus didn't know but for now the beach was full of folks playing happy families and it wamed his heart.

Marcus didn't expect to ever be a father. Wasn't cut out for it. Didn't want the commitment or responsibility for one thing. Yet a bit of him thought how great it would be.Taking his lad to football. Teaching him to ride a bike. He finished his ice cream and dismissed all thoughts of fatherhood. Knowing his luck he'd get a girl anyway. What a nightmare that would be.

Seagulls hung in the air over head, gliding in the breeze as Marcus leaned against the pier railings looking out to sea. For some reason his thoughts turned to Eliza. She had been twelve when he was born. More like a second mother than a sister. They hadn't had much in common but they had got on pretty well. His mother favoured her, but spoilt him too and if they argued would say to Eliza "you are old enough to know better. Let him be." Marcus would smile smugly. One nil to him!

He remembered a conversation he had had in a pub with a fellow United fan. They had been watching a match on Sky when Dave had said out of nowhere:

Has you sister ever had a bloke do you think?

Eliza?

Yeah. I saw her in the library today, while I was going to get the trillionth book on pregnancy and babies for my missus. I don't know what we ever talked about before she got pregnant. Honestly she's obsessed. I'm excited course I am but bloody hell, morning, noon and night that's all she talks about. Her mother is as bad. Phoning every morning and evening to see how she's feeling.

Anyway your sister was putting books away in the romance section and it just got me wondering if she had ever had romance of her own. She always seems so self contained and unreachable. Sorry mate, Dave suddenly seemed embarrased. Bit out of order talking about your sisters sex life.

Can't really say I've ever really thought about it he said then both men screamed

YES COME ON YOU REDS

As Wayne Rooney scored all but sealing the championship and banishing all thoughts of Eliza from the minds of them both.

Marcus thought about it now though. Was that where the seed had been sown? She was stuck up. Thought herself too good for anyone else. His mother had called it shyness. Whatever it was it had gradually begun to get on his nerves especially after a few pints. If he was honest he knew that it was only when he was in that state that he started to believe that she fancied him. Telling him he looked smart when he went out. Noticing when he had his hair cut. Doing him a packed lunch when she did hers.

A boat appeared on the horizon and disrupted his

thoughts. As did a golden retriever who bounded by him all but dragging a child behind him. The poor kid was hanging onto the lead for dear life. No match for the dog. Marcus smiled and headed into town. He'd have a look round maybe put a bet on then grab some fish and chips before he headed back. He wanted the day to last and with it the feeling of having no ties, no responsibilities. Some snobs might call it Weston Super Nightmere but it suited him. He picked up his helmet and sauntered back along the length of the pier. I am never going back to prison he said to himself. Never.

EDITH

Miss Garnet had died. Edith had known she would. Somehow though she died fulfilled Edith put down the book and unwrapped the sandwiches the carer had left her. How she had loved picnics. Sometimes they hadn't even gone out anywhere just picnicked in the garden. Eliza especially had thought it so exciting. She had been easily pleased as a child and still was really. Now it came to mind, she didn't really know what Eliza did with her time when she wasn't at work. I would love to go for one last picnic. If only she could face going down the stairs. She wondered would she chose the woods or the seaside?. The beach won. Maybe Burnham? There were wonderful stretches of sand there and it didn't get as crowded as Weston. There must be coach trips there in the summer. She was dreaming that's all. It wasn't going to happen. She was no Miss Garnet. She didn't have her courage or her depth. She didn't deserve a day out anyway. She wondered where Marcus had gone? He never told her what he did. Which was probably just as well. She did worry. He was so impatient and got angry so quickly. If only he could get help. Or meet someone he loved so much that he changed for them. She sighed that didn't happen did it? How many men and woman married thinking they could change their other half? A sudden wave of panic set in. Was it still Saturday? She reached across and put the radio back on waiting for a clue as to what time or what day it was. Were these sandwiches her lunch or supper. She couldn't remember. Rage at her inability to concentrate and hold on to reality flooded through her and she clenched her fists. Gradually the music from the radio calmed her. What did it matter what time or day it was. She didn't have plans and she wasn't going anywhere. She finished her sandwich and turned the radio back off. She would just rest for a bit and think about things later.

FIFTEEN

ELIZA

As she lay in bed that night. Eliza had found herself thinking about Pete and all he said to her. She wasn't in love with him or anything silly like that. But there was something very gently attractive about him. She had enjoyed his company. He had felt easy somehow and safe. Above all safe.

She had never had a serious boyfriend. Never felt the need really. She was a dreamer always on her own, but never on her own because of the world in her books. You should get out more her mother was always saying. Meet people. Nor be cooped up in your room all day. Why would I want to go out Eliza had thought when she was younger. She didn't have anything in common with the girls in her class. Even from a young age they only seemed to be interested in boys and clothes. Eliza could go anywhere in the world in her books. Reading or writing. She just loved words and never felt there was anything missing in her life. Well except her father and she had a gut feeling that he would never come back. She knew people talked about her. They thought she was stuck up and probably laughed at her expense. On the whole though Eliza didn't mind. She was odd, she admitted it. Or different as her counsellor had tried to get her to believe. She had fancied a few men along the way. There was a chap who came in to the library with his little girl and he was quite simply the most attractive man Eliza had ever set eyes on. He was about forty with brown hair, that stuck up, brown eyes and a smile that lit up the library. He was always smartly dressed and never seemed in a hurry. Others too from time to time had made her look twice. Though even if they had asked her out which they hadn't, she was far too shy. If anyone had chatted her up, and apart from a drunk one Christmas Eve, no one ever had, she would have been too self conscious to string one coherent sentence together. No she was ok with the truth that she was odd, different, whatever she was she didn't mind. Most of her didn't anyway.

She could barely talk to the man, with his daughter Charlie Foster, without going the colour of an over ripe sunset. She always tried to focus on the little girl, Alice or else she would get so tongue tied it was as if she had the worlds worst stutter.

She must have a hormone or two missing she thought sadly one day not to want to be out dating. She did get very upset once when Mr Fosters wife brought Alice in to the library one afternoon after school. She was the most irritable, rude, loud- mouthed woman Eliza had ever encountered. She pulled Alice along giving her no time to choose which book she wanted. She let the whole library know that she'd had to cancel an appointment because her poor excuse of a husband was still on the golf course. Eliza had been horrified. What on earth was such a nice man doing with such a dreadful woman?

She hated the word spinster. That was what she was though and what she would die as. Such morbid thoughts where did they come from? Just when her mind was beginning to clear and think normally, they crept in and sabotaged everything. She didn't want to think about death. It had preoccupied her thoughts for too long. For the first five years after Marcus had attacked her all she had wanted to do was to slip away quietly. Trying to care for her mum whose injuries had been so severe took all her strength even with the help from the carers.

The trip to Skye was in spite of everything all about life and hope. She knew Marcus was free and walking around the streets of Wellington, living in the house with their mother which still frightened her, but Skye was bigger than her fear. Yet it was almost time to leave. To go back to Gloucester. To the library. To the little bedsit which was her home. She had thought about staying on. The hotel had space for another three nights. She wouldn't even have to change rooms the receptionist had said. Her train ticket was booked though and her budget was spent. In any case would it be any easier to leave on Thursday than it would be to go tomorrow? She was due back at work on Wednesday so that was that. She suddenly felt trapped. The holiday had cost close to a thousand pounds. More money than she had ever spent in her life. She had saved hard and gone without so much. She just didn't have the resources to stay longer, but she didn't have the strength to leave either. I would like my ashes to be scattered here she thought. In this little cove with the seagulls looking on and the mountains like chief mourners in the background. God she was thinking about death again. STOP IT STOP

IT STOP IT she screamed to herself stifling sobs she was afraid those in the room next door might hear.

MARCUS

It had been a brilliant day but it was time to head back home. As he approached his bike he saw a gawky looking teenager inspecting it Seeing Marcus coming he said in a friendly sort of way

"Is that your bike?"

"Is it yours?" Marcus asked back

The boy grinned from ear to ear and shook his head.

"It must be mine then mustn't it so sod off."

"Alright mate I was just looking" The boy took a step back realising he may have made a mistake engaging Marcus in conversation

"Yeh well if I find a single mark on it I'm going to break your bloody legs."

Marcus saw the boy was scared now, his stupid baggy jeans so low that he was almost tripping over himself.

"I'm just going alright" He walked back towards the town as fast as he could without actually breaking into a run. He had some pride.

Marcus knew he had ruined the boys day. He could see why he had wanted to chat about the bike. What he couldn't quite understand was why he had gone for him. What had happened? He was just a kid. He had put the fear of God into the boy. But really did he care? No he didn't. Why the hell should he? Little git shouldn't have touched his bike.

He put his helmet on. Best he didn't have a son he thought as he headed back towards the A38 and home.

EDITH

Edith had been dozing for a while and when the front door slammed it jolted her whole body. It always did when Marcus was in a mood. He must have had a bad day. I hope he doesn't come in. I'd rather wait until the carer comes for my evening drink then have to face him in a thunderous mood. She needn't have worried. Marcus was barely in the house ten minutes before he was off out again. Edith breathed a huge sigh of relief and put the radio back on. She recognised the voice of the presenter but couldn't quite remember his name. It would come to her. Before the programme ended she would be sure to think of it. He was interviewing somebody or other. She had a very nice voice. Well spoken and with lots of interesting anecdotes about her life to share. Theresa someone. Edith took her mind off the radio for a minute and tried to think of something witty or amusing she could share about her own life. Nothing leapt out She would ponder on it a bit later. There must be some events worthy of sharing should she ever get the opportunity which she knew was extremely unlikely. No harm tucking one or two anecdotes away though just in case.

SIXTEEN

ELIZA

Monday morning came and it was tipping down. Eliza wondered if it was the islands gift to her, making it easier for her to leave. If the sun had been shining and the water had been like the gleaming expanse of jewels it had been on her first day her heart would have been even heavier. Breakfast, a taxi ride to Kyle of Lochaish, then a fourteen hour train journey back to Gloucester lay ahead of her. She had been up at three before the light had broken through and shadows had become shapes. Dawn had been a subdued affair but none the less beautiful for that. The mountains were hiding behind the mist or was it fog. She tried to remember the difference. She knew both were caused by the suspension of water droplets in the atmosphere close to the ground. Wasn't it fog if visibility was less than a thousand metres and mist if it was more? For some reason she wanted it to be mist. She felt closer to the mist. It spoke to her as it slipped in and out of the landscape. Hiding, revealing, hiding, revealing. Teasing her almost with its partial disclosures then shutting the door on its treasures just as she thought she might be able to peek at them again.

She was soaked through but she didn't care. She wanted to be with the island every last second. She wanted to imbibe every sight, every sound, every little thing about it she wanted to trap in her spirit. She wondered what Pete was doing. How must it have felt going back to an empty house again? She hoped he had a friendly neighbour who had been watering the plants and who have left a little note to say welome back. He deserved that. She hadn't given him her details so he couldn't contact her. She would email him though. She would give it a few days and then send a message thanking him. Thanking him for what though?. How would she ever put it into words? She got her little camera out of the inside pocket of her waterproof jacket and took a picture of the view in front of her. It was mostly just blurred shadows but there was just a tiny bit of light breaking through. She would send that to him if she could work out how to download it. She thought he would understand. She wasn't sure if she would go to Edinburgh next year. There were so many things to think through and the pit of her stomach had started to ache with the familiar dread and fear.

Eventually she dragged herself up and away from the waters edge over to the restaurant for her final breakfast. Sadness swamped her but she suddenly shouted to herself DAMMIT I am going to have porridge!. She didn't actually like porridge very much and she couldn't manage it all. It had just been a rather childish attempt to stick two fingers up at everything that dragged her down to a place she didn't want to be in . The pit that the psalmist talked about so much. Thomas and Abby came over and for one horrible moment she thought they were going to join her. Not today please not today she cried to herself. Please please leave me alone for these last moments.

"Hope you don't mind Eliza" Thomas said. "Only Pete mentioned that you were leaving this morning and so are we. We were wondering if we could offer you a lift to Inverness. Save you a taxi fare and one change on the train" Eliza's face nearly crumpled but she managed a thank you and meant it with all her being. "That's so kind of you" she mumbled. "No problem" Thomas said in the same business like tone he seemed to use for everything. "We will be heading out just before nine does that suit you?" "Oh its perfect timing" said Eliza "thank you again" "No trouble. Enjoy your porridge" he said as he went to join Abby at the table nearest the buffet.

Oh Pete, I should have known you would have had the last word. You kind kind man. She felt connected to him again and knew that even if she never met him again he had been a kind of angel. Like those she read about in stories, who stopped travellers on the road, journeyed with them for a while and imparted their wisdom, leaving them the same but totally changed. Given the age gap he was actually more like a father figure. What a shame he and his wife couldn't have children. He would have been brilliant. She buttered a last slice of toast, finished the remains of her coffee and headed back out into the rain, which now was actually more like drizzle for one last walk. Her sea gull was there. Not foraging but sitting on the water being gently carried up and down as each wave reached out foamy fingers towards the shore. You look after this place for me she said. Look after yourself too. Tears really were close now but the sadness was too deep and they remained tightly locked behind her eyes. How could beauty hurt so much? How could an island she had only been on for six days sink so deep into her soul. She had barely explored it. The two trips to Armadale and Portree her only excursions. She didn't have to see it all to know it all though. She would come back. She would hire a driver to show her more of the lochs and hills and mountains that it so carefully hid. The treasures that it kept safe. You can look but not touch it seemed to say. Brutal. Barren, Bleak. It was all those things. Yet. Yet it danced. It sang. It celebrated the very best of what it was to be alive. She took one last look and went to get her case. She couldn't bring herself to say goodbye to the seagull or to the Cuillins. It wasn't goodbye. Please God it wasn't.

Her key handed in she waited in the foyer for Thomas and Abby who put her case in the boot, started the engine and eased the car out of the car park onto the road back to Inverness

What was she going back to? She stared out of the window vaguely aware that Thomas and Abby were chatting about their dog who they would be collecting later from Abby's parents. Were they feeling it too she wondered? The wrench. The sense of something precious being slowly handed back over for others. Skye Bridge came into view and all too soon they were off the island and she was standing on a platform at Inverness station, cold and alone.

MARCUS

"You're not welcome here" The landlord had started as soon as Marcus had set foot in the pub "so clear out. You might think you got away with one the other night but we all know it was you who tried to burn the place down. Just as well you are such a useless piece of shit you made such a hash of it."

Marcus had come back from Weston in a foul mood. Even the journey back on his bike hadn't restored the feelings of contentment he had felt on the pier. It had been that wretched boy. Touching his bike, making him angry. It was his fault.

He couldn't settle so he had put his bike away and gone down the pub.

He glared at Billy, the diminutive landlord. He could take him out easily but with so many witnesses he would be done for.

"You might think you are a big man Marcus Grady" the smaller man continued on a roll "but in our books what you did makes you the lowest form of life. No one here was brave enough to say it to your face but I'm saying it now. Get out of this pub and if you come back I have friends who will make you wish you'd never been born."

Ah so that was it. Billy must be allowing drugs to be sold in there and he had the dealers minders covering his back and putting their filthy hands on anyone who didn't pay. No wonder the little prick was so full of himself. On his own he wouldn't have been able to stand up to his mother let alone him.

Shocked as he was. Marcus didn't let it show. He just slowly quietly put his money back in his pocket, turned to go then spat in the landlords face.

The whole pub had stood still watching to see what would happen. You could hear the proverbial pin drop. Some had edged closer to the door in case there was real trouble. The others had just stood and stared as though it were a scene from Eastenders. He did his best to sneer and walked out with as much arrogance and confidence as he could muster. An old bloke called Mickey was by the door and went as if to hold it open for him. At the last minute though he lost his nerve and stepped back leaving Marcus to open and close it himself.

That was the final straw. Ever since he had been back he had seen in peoples faces a mix of disgust and fear. It was a small town and most people stayed a long time once they moved in. They had long memories and they made harsh judgements. Marcus felt wronged it hadn't been his bloody fault that his mother had come at him with that knife trying to protect her precious Eliza. He served his time dammit. One of the cons he had got out with had told him as they had left the prison "Your sentence starts now." Marcus hadn't understood what he meant at the time. He understood now though.

He would have to move. He wouldn't mind that much. New start. New place. He'd have to sort his mother out. He could downsize to a two bedroom place somewhere like Weston and have a bit of cash to play with. Or he could go for a one bedroom place and off load his mother to social services. Or she could go and live with her precious Eliza. They deserved each other.They could pass their days moaning how unlucky they were to have such a terrible son and brother respectively. He was sure they would be very happy together.

That's what he would do. He would tell his mother tomorrow and start looking for a place just as soon as he had done the job for Mrs Wilkinson or whatever her name was. He could still come back and see Ellen from time to time. It wasn't running away, just doing what he should have thought of earlier, wiping the dust of this waste of space town off his boots and going somewhere where he could make something of himself.

Now he had a plan the anger which had almost consumed him died down. Maybe he would retrain as a mechanic. I mean how hard could that be? He would have to let his probation officer know and play it all by the book. Could work out alright though couldn't it? Marcus smiled to himself. His good humour restored. Nobody got the better of Marcus Grady. No one. He would get that waster of a landlord. Not today. Not tomorrow. Not the day after even. But he would get him.

EDITH

The door closed more quietly this time. For a moment Edith thought it must be the carer come back, maybe she had forgotten something. She was certainly scatty enough. It was Marcus though and he brought her the paper and asked how she was. Bloody suspicious that was he never asked how she was. Why would he? He didn't care.

Fine thanks she had said. A bit tired but alright. You ok?

Yes fine he had said. Fine. I need to run something by you tomorrow. I'm working all day but I'll pop in after and we can have a chat.

There it was. He was up to something. They never had chats and he never smiled at her like he had as he left her room.

She was seriously worried now. She wouldn't sleep a wink. If Marcus was making an effort to be nice to her then it was something seriously bad that he wanted to talk about. He couldn't be in trouble with the law or else he would be going back to prison. What plan could he possibly have hatched? It didn't enter her head for one moment that he might be going to sell the house. He had always lived here so the thought never crossed her mind. He seemed so cheerful so he couldn't be ill. He wasn't likely to tell her if he'd won millions on the lottery. She couldn't for the life of her think what it could be. She just knew she should be worried. If only the vicar would come again. It was probably selfish but it would help to know she was being prayed for and there was so much she wanted to talk to him about.

SEVENTEEN

ELIZA

After twelve hours, two changes and a fifteen minute walk from the station to her bedsit, Eliza was exhausted. The trains had all been packed and she had stood between Inverness and Edinburgh. She had reserved a seat but the man sitting in it was reluctant to move so she didn't make an issue of it. All she wanted by that stage was a bath and her bed. She had thought she might try and write on the journey back but everything had seemed so loud. Whether it was mobile phones ringing. Kids whingeing or babies crying they did so loudly. Her heart had been filled briefly with a sense of hope when the silhouette of the trees on Mayhill, then the illuminated Gloucester Cathedral tower came into view. The respite was brief though. She loved the Cathedral and the tower always reminded her of a wonderfully decorated cake It wasn't as old as the Cuillin mountains but it had that same solid sanctity about it. Occasionally she went and listened to Evensong. She loved to hear the psalms sung and the choirboys voices and the organ produced notes that hung in the air and drew her away from herself to an otherness far greater than she could name or hold on to. She never lingered, always leaving before the end thus avoiding the clergy and other worshippers. She needed the anonymity. She hadn't been for a while she realised. Maybe she would go one evening in the week after work, might help her face and cope with the transition from island to city. It would be school holidays in a month or so and the choir would finish for their summer break. A lot of the services were said then rather than sung. Though some visiting choirs did deputise. She never went when the choir was away. It was the music that drew her and held her. For once words weren't enough. They seemed to get lost in the vastness of the vaulted nave. It was the music that wrapped itself around them and gave them susbstance and power.

Once in, Eliza couldn't face unpacking. In the end she couldn't even face a bath. It was nearly midnight and she was well and truly done in.

MARCUS

The day had gone well. Mrs Wilkinson had been pleased with his work. Shown him where everything was and told him to make tea and coffee whenever he liked. She had bought some fruit cake for him as well. You need to keep your strength up she'd said.Big chap like you. The old girl was a bit of a fruit cake herself if you asked Marcus. Seemed to spend the whole day talking to herself. Still, wasn't his business. Going through her stuff wasn't his business either but he would be doing that right enough. The night before he had finalised his plan to move. His mother had a choice, social services or Eliza. He didn't care which. She wasn't coming with him that's all that mattered. He would tell anyone he got to know in Weston that he had moved because his mother had died. It wouldn't be much of a lie anyway. Most of the time a dying duck in a thunderstorm had more about it than she did, lying there feeling sorry for herself. Lots of people lost limbs they didn't take to their beds though did they? He knew she had a bit of a knock on her head too but even so.

He thought of catching the bus home. It was only a few stops though, so in the end he decided to walk. Give him time to think how to phrase things with his mother. He stopped momentarily outside his old primary school. The Iron Duke himself had donated £50 in 1850 to help found it. He wouldn't beat about the bush but he would choose his words carefully and try not to upset her too much. Didn't want her crying all night. He needed to be up early again in the morning for work and she was his mother after all.

In fact the decision to walk took away all time from him and he would need no words.

Whether he was pushed or slipped. Whether the car mounted the kerb or not wasn't clear. The fact was that it hit Marcus full on and his body lay in the road as ugly in death as it had been in life. Eye witnesses were too shocked to remember their own names let alone agree on what they had seen. The car didn't stop and a car coming the other way had hit Marcus as well. The lady driver who had only just passed her test was inconsolable and the severity of his injuries added to the hideous nature of the incident. As his blood trickled onto the tarmac and screams hung in the air an ambulance pulled up. It was too late though. Far too late.

.

EDITH

He would be home soon. It must be time. It would be soon she knew it would. As hard as she had tried she had not been able to come up with a reason why Marcus would want to talk to her. He didn't involve her in any of his decisions. She didn't know how much money he had or didn't have. Had he met someone she wondered? Was that it?. Was he going to get married. Was a woman going to be moving in with them. It sounded possible. The only flaw was that he wouldn't bother to talk to her about it. The woman would just appear. Maybe the woman was pregnant? But he had only just got out of prison. Couldn't he just come home and put her out of her misery. Whatever it was it couldn't be as bad as the turmoil in her head. could it?

She heard the door open and she let out a gasp. Oh Vicar you've come. Thank God I need to talk to you before Marcus gets home. We'll need to be quick.

EIGHTEEN

ELIZA

The phone call came just as Eliza was getting up. Tired as she was, she had had a wretched night. In the end she had got out of bed at seven and made herself a coffee. She was just finishing getting dressed when she heard her mothers voice on the other end of the phone. She had left her number with the local vicar for emergencies so he must have given it to her mother.

"I'm sorry I didn't get back until late last night, but I'll come straight away" she said and put down the receiver.

It wasn't until she had gone on the train. That what she had heard sunk in. Hard as she tried she couldn't feel a single thing. Not even relief. She didn't want Marcus to be dead. She didn't want him to be in her life. But she had never wished him dead. It was herself she had tried to release from life's grip. Her mother hadn't really made much sense. The vicar who had just been coming out of church when the accident happened, was with her and he filled her in with the details. Hit and run. Killed instantly. Could she come and identify him at the hospital morgue?

She would do that first. It wouldn't seem real otherwise. She'd only seen one dead body before and that had been Richard's. Marcus' father. He hadn't really looked dead.

Just not quite alive with skin like rubber and an expression on his face that didn't suit him. Though she couldn't have told you what the expression was. She wondered what Marcus would look like. She hadn't seen him since the day in court when he had been sentenced. He had refused to plead guilty, which would have spared her the ordeal of having to give evidence. He had said he hadn't meant to hurt their mother but that she had come at him with a knife and he had acted in self defence. Regards her, he had said..... She couldn't bear to think again about what he had said. The jury had taken barely twenty minutes to find him guilty and the judge had imposed the maximum sentence that he could. It had been Marcus' arrogance that had been his undoing and his assassination of her character. No one had believed his version of events and it had been obvious to everyone that her and Ediths suffering wouldn't end with his imprisonment. It had been touch and go for a while whether their mother would even survive. Although the loss of her leg just above the knee had got the most headlines.it was the blow to her head as she had fallen down the stairs with Marcus on top of her crushing her that had been life threatening. She had been unconscious for ten days suffering irreversible brain damage. It affected her memory mostly but she had had excruciating headaches for months afterwards and the depression that had overhelmed her had never quite lifted. Physically Eliza knew she had got off lightly and the brusies had faded in time. It wasn't her physical wounds that hurt though. It was the ones inside.

EDITH

"What do you mean he's dead. Edith exclaimed. "He can't be he's coming home to tell me something. In fact I've been worrying about it all day. I think he might have got a girl pregnant." The vicar who she now remembered was called David Barnes was in his fifties` and had been parish priest in Wellington for the past six years. He knew the familys history and had called to see her every quarter. In between one of his pastoral visitors had popped in. He had brought her communion in the early days. She hadn't wanted to receive the host after the first Christmas. She knew she didn't deserve it. He had tried to reassure her but in the end they had just talked and he had given her a blessing. She was more comfortable with that.

He took her hand.

"I know its a lot to take in Edith he had said .But Marcus isn't coming back. He's dead. It's a terrible shock I know. He was hit by a car. He didn't suffer. He wouldn't have known anything about it." She saw the vicar flinch. That was a lie she thought, He might be a man of God but he couldn't know if that was true could he? She wondered if Marcus had seen the car out of the corner of his eye and known it was going to hit him. Had there been time for terror? For a calling out? Had his life passed before him? Or had he literally been alive thinking one thing one second and dead the next.

"Where is he now then?" she asked trying to hold on to the thought that he might still be alive . She remembered the vicar being there last night but thought it had been a dream. Didn't the police come too?

"He's in the hospital." the vicar said gently

"Elizas on her way. So you are not to worry. She will sort everything out. The police will be back later. They will need to ask you a few questions. The carer is downstairs too. She's making you a hot drink." Was it her imagination or was he speaking to her as though she was a three year old? Bewilderment was making breathing difficult and it seemed so hot in the room.

You mean he was killed outside his old school? Thank God the children had long since gone home. The sight of a broken body was more than anyone should have to see let alone a child.

Apparently the vicar told her the police were still taking statements and trying to piece together what had happened. All the witnesses had said that it had happened so quickly and all they really remembered was the sound of his body hitting the car. She wondered if anyone had held his hand as he died. He was so many things but she couldn't bear the thought of him dying like some magpie or rabbit that was just left on the side of the road for everyone to stare at.

NINETEEN

ELIZA

They had done their best at the morgue to make the experience as least distressing as possible but still she felt sick. It had been nearly midday by the time she had arrived and the attendant along with a lovely police woman, Ruth had said she could view the body from behind a glass screen. Ruth explained that he had taken the full force of the impact on his upper body so they wouldn't show her his whole face just the one side that wasn't so badly damaged.

"Are you ready?"

Eliza took a deep breath, then closed her eyes as tight as she could for what seemed an age. They didn't rush her and when she opened her eyes she looked up quickly and as quickly looked away again. She knew it was him. She found her throat was so tight that she couldn't speak. Her tongue was trapped somewhere in her mouth and her whole face ached as if in sympathy with the face before her. It was the face of the boy she had helped bring up. It was the face of the man who had raped her. It was Marcus.

She nodded and as the attendant covered Marcus up again. Ruth genty took her by the elbow and guided her back out in to the fresh air. They stood side by side until eventually Ruth spoke.

"I won't ask if you are alright, but is there anything I can do?" Eliza had temporarily forgotten the woman was there and was confused for a moment. She tried to organise the nothingness that had swamped her head. Her whole body felt numb and she could barely focus her eyes on the officer.

"Take as long as you need and I'll be back in a moment" Ruth disappeared back into the building and true to her word was back alongside Eliza before she had barely even registered that she had gone.

She was carrying two polystyrene cups. "I don't know what you usually drink but I got you a tea with two sugars. Here hold it. You look frozen."

Eliza took hold of the cup and its warmth gradually seeped through her hands into her body and she began to think again.

"Could you order a taxi for me to Wellington." Eliza eventually managed to say.

"No need" said Ruth "I'll take you myself. It's only twenty minutes and I have to report back anyway."

She looked at Eliza and said softly

"I know what happened. I think you are very brave coming here."

Such genuine kindness always broke Eliza.

"I don't know how I am supposed to feel." she said desperate to feel something. Anything would be better than the paralysis that had taken hold of her body.

"Feelings will come later. Don't try too hard and don't fight whatever comes when it does hit you."

"I thought I would feel a massive sense of relief. Although I have never said it, there have been times when I wished him gone. Not dead just gone.Now he is I just don't know what to do" She was like a child needing the reassurance of a parent.

She sipped her tea. "I must get to mum though. She will be in a terrible state. She isn't well."

"I know" said Ruth. "She will be pleased to see you. The doctor gave her a sedative last night so she might still be a bit groggy. She kept telling the vicar that Marcus couldn't be dead because he was on his way to tell her something important. Poor woman has been through enough. You both have without this. "

Eliza sat in the back of the police car and Ruth left her to her thoughts. She tried to look out of the window to get her bearings back. Everything was a blur though. People going to work, going shopping. A day like any other day. Funny how the world just kept on turning, time just kept on passing. Whatever was happening in peoples lives there was a bigger picture, a greater canvas and that never seemed to notice if anyone was missing or hurting. She was hurting, but not for Marcus she didn't think. Or was she? Was she grieving for the little boy who had been so proud when she had given him his first pet rabbit? I've called him Arthur he had said. His father had sneered but she and Mum had told him what a wonderful strong name it was. Later he had been even more excited when Fred Rimmer the old chap down the road had told him that Arthur meant 'high ground' He told everyone who would listen about his new knowledge and his new best friend.

Or was it that she couldn't let herself be glad he was dead? Was she suppressing her real feelings? Was she glad? She didn't know. Except she did. Of course she was glad he was dead. Or was she? She would have been on the train when it happened.Whereabouts she wondered? Leeds? Derby? Birmingham? She closed her eyes again and it seemed like an instant when Ruth pulled up outside the house.

"Would you like me to come in with you?" she asked.

"No" Eliza whispered. "It's alright."

Ruth told her the carer had stayed on. "She assured us she would wait until you arrived. Good of her."

"Everyone has been good. Thank you." Eliza said without feeling. Her words were coming out on their own and she could only watch as though it were all happening to somebody else.

"I'll be back in touch when we have some more news the police woman continued. "For now do the simple things like eat and drink and try to get some sleep when you can."

EDITH

Edth had had the strangest dream . She had dreamt that Marcus was dead. He wasn't of course but it had disturbed her. She had woken with a terrible headache and nothing seemed quite in focus or real. Lara with her bright red head hair knocked and came in. Eliza's on her way. She will be here any minute.

Eliza? For a moment Edith had to wrack her brain to think who Eliza was. Then in horror as understanding crept back into the place it had previously vacated. She screamed NO she mustn't come. Marcus is here. Tell her she mustn't come.

Lara was out of her depth but as she struggled for words she heard the front door open and all but flew downstairs.

TWENTY

ELIZA

"Hi" she said "I'm Lara.You must be Eliza"

"Yes" Eliza said and held out her hand for Lara to shake. "Thank you so much for staying on. I will make sure you are reimbursed for your time." "It's no problem the young carer said "Your mum is a bit confused though. She hasn't really understood that Marcus is dead. It's all been a shock. "

"I'll go up and see her? Can you do extra hours Thursday and Friday too? Yes sure my mobile number is in the kitchen by the fridge. Just let me know when you need me". Eliza smiled gratefully at the girl and turned towards the stairs.

With each step the feeling of nausea and dread increased until she had to hold on to the bannister rail to steady herself. Deep breaths she said to herself and knocked on the door.

It had only been three months since Mothers Day when Eliza had last seen her mother. The change in her though was shocking. Her face was grey and etched with new lines. Her eyes were filled with fear and she seemed to have shrunk. All of a sudden, the bed looked far too big for her

"Hi Mum its me" Eliza said and went over to kiss Edith on her forehead. "Eliza you must go" Edith warned her. "Marcus is here". Eliza pulled up the chair closer to the bed and took her mothers papery thin hand. "Mum. Marcus is dead. He was involved in an accident yesterday. A car hit him. He's gone. I'm sorry Mum but he's gone." Edith stared at Eliza for a moment and then dropped her chin on her chest. A wail escaped from somewhere so deep inside her that it sounded as if it must have ripped out blood and muscle as it had escaped from her mouth. She didn't cry but rocked herself back and forwards. Eliza sat transfixed. The hideous noise had chilled her to the bone. Was it grief? Anger? Relief?

Gradually her mother stopped her rocking motion and said simply "Are you here to stay?"

"I'll stay tonight. Then I have to go back to Gloucester. I've spoken to my boss and he has asked if I could work Thursday, Friday and Saturday morning. Then I can take the whole of next week off. It will give him time to get some cover. I'll make us a sandwich and then while you have a rest I will pop and see the vicar to arrange things. There will need to be an inquest but we should be able to hold a service next week hopefully. Is that ok with you?"

"A service ?" Edith was puzzled again. "Yes of course. We will need to have a funeral won't we. That's what you do when people die isn't it?" Edith paused then asked quietly

"Is he really dead?" "He is mum I'm sorry. . "I'm sorry too" Edith said. "Sorry for everything." "Now don't go blaming yourself." The words came out a bit more sternly than she had meant. "You did everything you could for him and for me. So why don't you just rest your eyes for a minute while I pop down to the kitchen."

After lunch Eliza left her mother dozing and went into town to meet with the vicar who she brought back with her to see Edith again. While he sat with her Eliza went into her old room to see about some bedding for the night.

EDITH

"Will Marcus be in hell now?" Edith asked Father David as he suggested she call him.

"I don't know I honestly don't."

"What's your best guess then" Edith said angrily. What was the point of a vicar who didn't know anything about heaven and hell?

"My best guess is that God is merciful and sees into the very depths of the human heart drawing out the best that is there. Marcus did something terrible, but my hope, my belief is that forgiveness is always available even at the last moment."

Edith more frustrated than ever ranted that Marcus wouldn't have had time in his last moment would he? He didn't know the car was going to hit him. He didn't know it was his now or never moment to talk to God.

She could see that the vicar was struggling trying to pry out both for himself and Edith words that might offer some hope without being airy fairy. "We don't know what happens at the point of death" the troubled vicar went on. "We so want absolutes at times like this. We just don't have them We have Jesus' promises in Johns Gospel that there are many rooms in his Fathers house. We have his conversation with the dying thief who he promises will be welcomed into the Kingdom. We have to trust Edith or else we end up putting ourselves through a kind of hell. As hard as it is. You have to let go of Marcus. You can do that despairing because of the things he did. Or you can do trusting that God is able even in death maybe to transform people and draw out the best of all they were or could have been. Gods love is so much greater than ours. I know it must seem unfair to victims even offensive to them maybe, I have to believe though that every man and every woman has one last chance to choose life. To face up to the consequences of their actions and to embrace forgiveness. "

His words hadn't really satisfied Edith and she wondered if they had really satisfied him He was sincere she could see that and had been ordained for twenty three years Yet every year that went by he said he seemed to understand less and less. His faith held strong but he had fewer and fewer answers to the questions of Why? That were tossed at him. He didn't know why the innocent suffered. He never had and in this life, his one certainty was that he never would and would have to live with the tension of faith and mystery. Edith wanted answers but she could see she wasn't going to get them so she went quiet.

"We can sit down next week with your daughter and talk about what music you would like for Marcus the vicar had gone on and which reading. We will pray for Marcus at the service. All of us together. "

Edith tried not to close her eyes which felt heavier and heavier. It wouldn't be much of a service would it? Only her and Eliza would be there. In truth she wasn't sure if she would be able to manage it. Eliza had felt she should try though. That she would always regret it if she didn't go.

David said he was hoping they could arrange it for the following Friday early afternoon. He would take them in his car. There was room for the wheelchair in the boot. He would bring them straight back and go on to Evensong. Taunton crematorium was less than twenty five minutes away from Wellington. They would be there and back in under two hours. Lara the young carer had told him that she would go to the service to show support . There would also be a police presence just in case the driver of the first car that had hit Marcus who still hadn't come forward went along to the service out of guilt. Apparently,it happened like that sometimes

He sat and read the twenty third psalm to Edith as she dozed. How many souls had those words soothed over the centuries. She reminded him a bit of his own mother who had died a little under two years ago. So many fears. So many questions. So much anguish. He flicked through the pages of his well worn Bible until he came to the passion story and read again Jesus heartfelt cry from the cross 'Eloi Eloi, lama sabachthani. My God My God why have you forsaken me?

It was Good Friday in this house. He closed his Bible and prayed with all his heart for a glimpse of Easter Morning for them too. For a rolling away of the stone from the tomb that these two women had spent most of the last eight years in.

TWENTY-ONE

ELIZA

Eliza had heard Father David reading the passion story and praying but must have dozed for over an hour. When she got up and checked on Edith, she was still asleep. The police were coming later to have a look in Marcus' room. They didn't think he had been mown down deliberately but with his history and some of the less than legal deals he had been involved in, they wanted to go through his papers just in case he had received any threatening letters. Or if they was any evidence that he owed some serious money. They may have just meant to put the frighteners on and it had gone wrong. Until the driver of the car came forward if they ever did, they wanted to cover every possibility. Ruth was one of the police officers who came along with a younger blond constable. They were only in his room for about twenty minutes and after a cursory look in the garage where they found only his bike and painting and decorating supplies and equipment, they left, but not before Ruth had asked how Edith was bearing up and if she had managed to to eat. "Do you know any more about what happened?" Eliza asked her.

"I'm afraid not. Very confused accounts from the people at the scene. They can't even agree on the colour of the car that hit him. Though it was definitely dark and long. So we are probably looking for an estate. We are checking all the local garages but it all takes time. I'm sorry I know it's hard when you have so many questions going round in your head. I'm just off to see the lady who was driving the second car again. I think I mentioned that the force of the impact with the first vehicle threw Marcus into the path of a car coming the other way. The driver had not long passed her test and is completely distraught. We have tried to tell her that Marcus was almost certainly dead before she hit him. In her mind though she has killed a man. She wanted to come round and tell you how sorry she was but I persuaded her against that."

"Oh thank you," Eliza said relieved. "Mum wouldn't cope with that and neither would I. I have hardly got enough energy to deal with my own emotions. Or lack of them. I don't need anyone else's pain. I'm sorry if that sounds selfish." "It sounds real," Ruth said. "And you don't need to apologise." Eliza thought for a moment. "Maybe I could write a letter sometime just reassuring her that we don't in any way blame her."

"That would be an amazingly generous thing to do and I will try to reassure her on your behalf." Ruth said.

"How do you cope with eveyones stuff? You had me at the morgue. You've come here, now you are going to see someone else who is in a terrible place. How do you stay sane?"

Ruth smiled. "I have three year old twins. A boy and a girl. Sammy and Rosie. They are my lifeline and my husband of course.He's in the force too so understands. Sometimes it all gets on top of me and I have to take time out. Last year a toddler was killed in a house fire and I could hardly bear to leave my two each morning. They were about the same age as the little girl who died. It does get to you but you just have to learn to manage. Its the courage of the people you meet that often gives you the strength to go on. You've managed."

Eliza hung her head. "No I haven't not really."

"You are still here. Fighting and trying to put the past in a place where it can't destroy your future. You are braver than you think."

Suddenly she thought of Pete and the words he had said to her. Was she really through the worst? Could there really be a little space in the crowded world for someone like her? She closed the door behind the officers and went back up to her mother. "Why don't you get out of bed for a little while?" she said. "I could carry the little table up and we could have a bit of supper together. I've put some jackets in the oven. They should be ready soon."

EDITH

"We always used to have jackets on bonfire night do you remember and a little packet of sparklers between us." "It was one of my favourite nights of the year," Eliza replied smiling at the memory. Soon got too tame for Marcus though didn't it. Once he was grown up he would go off into Taunton with his mates to the big bonfire at the Rugby Club.

"Where did I go wrong Eliza? Where?" Tears flowed down Ediths face and Eliza let her cry, holding her hand as she sobbed. "It wasn't your fault Mum. His dad didn't help and he just got in with the wrong crowd. Quick pickings versus hard work. It was a no brainer as far as Marcus was concerned. He kept his painting and decorating up but once Richard died and he was the man of the house he changed. He liked the power. He liked having a bike everyone else could only dream of owning. He became a bully I suppose. He was still Marcus but a man not a boy anymore. We lived in the same house and day after day said 'good morning' and 'good night' but we weren't a family. He outgrew us. He gradually slipped through our fingers." Eliza stopped. That was as far as she felt able to go. The mother and daughter had never spoken of that night and were never likely to.

TWENTY TWO

ELIZA

True to her word Lara, had stayed with Edith as much as she could, allowing Eliza to go back to Gloucester to work and to collect some more of her things. She had been in such a daze when the call about Marcus had come she had just grabbed some clothes from her case stuffed them in a holdall and rushed out for the train.

She was on the train again now heading to Taunton. She would get a bus from there to Wellington and stay until the following Sunday. There were some big decisions to make about Mums future. It didn't appear that Marcus had made a will. So once probate was sorted the house would be Ediths. It surely wasn't the best option for her to stay there. So many memories and so impractical for her needs. Eliza sighed and looked out of the window again at the Somerset countryside. Sheep stood in a field. Seagulls far too far away from the sea along with the jet black rooks scoured the immaculately ploughed land. What worries did they have? She had brought a book to read on her journey but had read and re read the first page so many times without taking in a single word that she had given up and put it back in her bag. She had too much in her head. Not just thoughts but a new sort of heaviness that assaulted her until she ended up almost in a trance.

Two hours later and she was back at the house . She called up the stairs and Lara came down to greet her. "Your mums really confused again sorry. She can't seem to concentrate for more than a moment and she has been asking after you."

"Thanks Lara," Eliza said and handed her an envelope with her additional wages in. "I hope you aren't too exhausted." "No its alright," the young girl said though she looked totally drained. Grief was exhausting for everyone who came into his presence however remotely. "I'll put the kettle on for you, Oh and a couple of cards came through the door. They are on the side."

Eliza made her way again up the stairs. The blue carpet really needed replacing. The whole house needed a facelift. She would have to talk to her mother but not today.

EDITH

Whether she opened her eyes or closed them Ediths head buzzed as if there were a million angry bees in it. It puzzled her why the bees would be angry. She had loved watching them slurping up their nectar from the flowers in her garden. There had been that book too. Now what was it called ? Oh yes The Secret Life of Bees? She wondered what they did in their secret life but she couldn't remember. She just knew that the noise of the ones that had somehow got into her head was deafening and she couldn't think or sleep or remember all the things she knew she was supposed to be in control of. She was going mad. She was sure of it. Even her food tasted bitter and she had no idea whether it was day or night. The police had been again and asked some questions. What kind of mother must they have thought she was? She knew nothing about Marcus' life. What he did. What he owned. It was as if he was a total stranger.

She couldn't quite grasp that it was Eliza standing at the door. When she was sure the person standing there wasn't just a figment of her imagination she cried. "I thought you were dead too," she sobbed as Eliza held her. Eliza too was close to tears. Her mother was disappearing in front of her eyes. Each time she saw her there seemed to be less and less of her. She wasn't yet seventy but the aging process had wrapped itself around her mothers mind and body and like some sort of parasite was draining away her life blood and sanity day by day.

"I had to go back to work Mum, but I'm here now. Lara has put the kettle on and I'll make us both a nice cup of tea." Where would the world be without cups of tea Eliza thought. She was amazed at how calm she was able to be. She wanted to scream at God or the universe or the man in the moon. Someone, anyone who could ease her mums agony.

Edith stared at her daughter as if trying to recognise her. It was all so dark. She was cold and she needed to know what it was she was supposed to be doing. Marcus was dead, surely she was supposed to be doing something?.

In the end she just said "I don't know what to do." "I know mum but you don't have to do anything. Not today anyway."

What a relief Edith thought, nothing to do today. A sudden panic swept through her and she all but shouted, but what about tomorrow ? What do I have to do then?

She vaguely knew that she was losing control of herself. Her voice. Her thoughts. Everything inside her had speeded up but somehow she was going slower. There would be a big crash soon. She just knew there would.

She hung on to her mug of tea as if it were a life raft. Drink your tea she said to herself. Drink your tea.

Eliza was talking again and holding up a card. It had a beautiful picture of a rose on the front. It wasn't her birthday was it?

It's from St Johns Eliza said and read the card out:

'Dear Mrs Grady

We were so sorry to hear about the sudden death of your son. We are praying for him and for you and Eliza. With our fondest best wishes and sincere sympathy Father David, the pastoral team and all at St Johns.'

She wasn't Mrs Grady she had never married Richard. She was Mrs Harris and what was the use of praying for Marcus? Bit late now wasn't it? He was dead.

She was about to say that to Eliza when a sudden thought crept into her mind. If Marcus was in hell and the congregation prayed for him. Perhaps he would get transferred to heaven. Yes that must be it. She smiled and for the first time since she had heard the news she felt maybe things might be alright. She would just close her eyes for a bit. Eliza wouldn't mind.

TWENTY THREE

ELIZA

The second card had been addressed to her alone. It was from Ruth the police officer who had met her at the morgue. She said she had been thinking of her and could she pop round on Sunday. It was her day off but there was something quite urgent she needed to discuss. Nothing Eliza should worry about but could she call about ten. She had added her mobile phone number in case this wasn't convenient.

Maybe they know who knocked Marcus down Eliza thought but why would she come round on her day off? She left her mother sleeping and went across the landing to her old room. It looked as though Marcus had been in there moving things about. She hadn't noticed that before. Or maybe the police had been in there. She had left the bed made from last week It was only eight more nights she told herself. She supposed she would have to clear out Marcus' stuff. Maybe she could get someone in to do it. Her heart sank. No she would have to do it and she would have to talk to her mother about moving. It was so cruel. Her illness, her confusion. She was alive and yet she wasn't, not really, not living. She would make an appointment to see her mums doctor. Was she getting steadily worse or was it the shock of Marcus death? Would she regain some of her ability to know and understand what was happening? She probably needed a new mental health assessment. Oh Eliza groaned. It was just all too overwhelming. Too heavy a weight for her to carry. She put her head in her hands. She would think about it tomorrow. Not today.

EDITH

All of a sudden Edith was dreaming a lot. A mix of absurdity and reality. She had been at the supermarket but everythng kept falling out of her basket. She asked Marcus to help but he had piled things higher and higher. Things they didn't need or even like. Eventually she had collapsed under the weight of it all but nobody noticed. Everyone who went by added more and more items. Heavy things like sacks of potatoes and tins of beans. She kept calling out but the words got trapped inside her throat and no one could hear. Finally Marcus had come and hauled her out from underneath the tons of food. He had been so angry. "Making a bloody show of yourself. You make me sick!." She had been left on her own sitting in the middle of one of the aisles not knowing what to do. She couldn't afford to buy everything so she knew she would have to put it all back on the shelves. She had woken up at that point and remembered clear as day the time Marcus had deliberately pulled all the boxes of cereals off the shelves because she wouldn't let him have his own way. Oh Marcus she cried out. What happened to you? What did I do wrong?

She was relieved to see Eliza who she thought looked pale. I'm sorry I'm such a burden to you she had said and meant it. Don't be silly you're not a burden you're my mum. Edith knew she was a burden though. She was a burden to herself so how could she not be to everyone else as well?

TWENTY FOUR

ELIZA

Ruth arrived spot on ten. She was carrying a bunch of roses. "They are for you" she said. "The twins helped me cut them this morning. They have gone to their Gran today so my husband and I are going out to lunch."

"You are so thoughtful" Eliza said as she took them from the police officer." I told them that they were for a lady who was going through a tough time and that flowers made people feel better." Eliza was getting closer and closer to tears. She had gone years and years without being able to cry and now she could barely get through a morning without welling up. She found a little vase and put the roses on the kitchen table.

"Shall we talk in here? Ruth asked. "Yes yes that's fine" Eliza said. "Would you like a coffee?" "Not for me" answered Ruth. "But do make yourself one." "I'll wait and have one with mum later. Making her drinks is about the useful thing I can do. She's really struggling and its so hard to watch. I feel so helpless and utterly useless."

"Don't be too hard on yourself Eliza. The best thing you can do for your mum is show her that you are getting on with your life. That you haven't been beaten."

Eliza tried to take reassurance from the police officers

words. She seemed much more petite out of uniform, dressed in a casual pair of beige trousers and a simple patterned white blouse with a silk scarf around her neck. Eliza thought she was beautiful. She herself had her usual full length skirt on and a long sleeved blouse buttoned up to the neck. She was only a few years older than the woman opposite her but she felt as if she was from another era.

Ruth pulled an envelope out of her shoulder bag. "I want to show you something Eliza. I found it when we were searching through Marcus' things. I've hung on to it for a few days. I just couldn't decide what to do. I could have passed it on. Or I could have left it for you to find. Only it requires a decision and I felt it would be a hard one for you to make on your own."

She handed the envelope over to Eliza. "It wasn't sealed so I had a look inside, just in case it was relevant or suggested a motive for murder."

"What do you mean a motive for murder?"

"It is his last wishes and had someone known they were to benefit from his death they might have speeded the process up by knocking him down."

"You have to think of so many different things don't you." "Sadly some of the people we deal with aren't exactly pillars of the community. It is depressing sometimes but there are more good folks out there than bad ones."

The envelope was adressed to 'whom it may concern on the occasion of my death.' I would like this to be treated as my will please. Elizas fingers were trembling as she pulled out the piece of plain A5 paper.

It read

I MARCUS GRADY being of sound mind hereby declare that this house, all its contents, all cash in it and my bike in the garage, should be given to the RSPCA.

NOT my family

Thank you

SURPRISE SURPRISE!!!!

It was signed and dated.

Eliza was beyond being able to form words. Eventually she said simply

"What will happen to mum? How am I going to tell her?"

"You don't have to tell her Eliza. You don't have to follow his wishes. It isn't countersigned and I am sure you could contest it in a court of law.

Or... "she paused

"Or you could just rip it up."

Eliza looked horrified. "I can't do that."

"You can and I strongly encourage you to do exactly that. If not for yourself, then for your mother. She could move into a place where she could be cared for and have company. The proceeds from the sale of the house would help her so much. She deserves that. You deserve that."

Eliza mind was in a turmoil. "Isn't it a criminal offence? You are a police officer you shouldn't be telling me to do this?"

"I'm a police officer and a woman who has an inkling of what you are going through. The letter was an act of spite on Marcus' part. It was probably aimed more at you than at his mother. He would surely have expected to outlive her."

"He should have outlived me too. I'm twelve years older than he was "

"He should have, but he hasn't and I think his better self would want to provide for his mother. "

Eliza put the paper back into the envelope. She couldn't bear to touch it. Did he really hate them both that much? Did he still blame them for his prison sentence? For ruining his life?

"You can see why I didn't want you to have to make the decision alone" said Ruth. "If you destroy the letter you have to let it go inside too. You can't carry guilt around inside you for what you've done. Do you want some time to think?"

Just then, Eliza heard Ediths weak voice calling her. She looked at Ruth and as she got up from the table to go to her mother she said quietly. "Please take the letter away." Ruth picked up the envelope and put her hand on Eliza's shoulder. "It's the right thing" she said. "Even if it's wrong. It's the right thing."

Eliza picked up the vase of roses and for the thousandth time went up to her mother who was calling her name.

EDITH

"They can't stay in my room" Edith said as soon as she saw the roses. "They will just attract more bees and there are enough in my head already." Eliza was taken aback, "but they are beautiful and their scent is just gorgeous."

136

"Take them away", she was getting was agitated now and waited for Eliza to do as she was told and take the roses to her own room.

"I would have thought you would have had more sense Eliza than bringing those things in here." Eliza apologised and then said "you called me was there something you needed. Would like to get out of bed and sit in the chair?"

Edith wracked her brain again. She couldn't begin to remember why she had called her daughter. She allowed Eliza to help her into her chair and then asked. How many days there were before the funeral. Its Sunday today Eliza said and the funeral is Friday so five days. Five days. Edith tried to bolt down how long that was in terms of mornings and nights. Quite a long time she thought that was alright then.

"The hairdresser, is coming on Wednesday to give you a trim. Its grown quite long hasn't it?" Had it? Whenever she looked in the mirror she didn't seem to have any hair at all. It was all plastered to the top of her head. The carers usually combed it for her. It hurt sometimes but she never let on. They meant well. "Should I wear a hat do you think?" "If you would like to . I'll get your things out later and you can choose what outfit you would like to go in." Go where Edith thought suddenly confused. Where were they going? She tried to rewind her morning to see if there was a clue in the conversations she'd had. She hadn't had any though had she?

"I'll pop downstairs and make some tea for us" Eliza had said slipping out of the room leaving Edith to play a game with herself of guessing where they were going. It might be fun she thought. Things were looking up.

TWENTY FIVE

ELIZA

The day of the funeral had come all too soon and yet not soon enough. The wait felt torturous. Made her wonder what it must be like for prisoners on death row. As the day of their execution drew closer. Time both dragged and flew by and she just wanted it to be over with.

Father David had come early and carried Edith down the stairs. It had been an ordeal for them both, but Eliza had finally managed to get her mother dressed in her two piece suit. It was a pale silvery blue and Eliza chose that moment to give her mother the scarf she had bought on Skye which she wrapped round her neck and which Edith kept fingering all day. The suit was a bit too big but it was respectable enough and her mother would be in the wheelchair with a blanket over her most of the time. To get through the service, Eliza, who wore an ankle length black skirt with a pale cream blouse and cream cardigan had pretended she was somewhere else. She closed her eyes and pictured the mountains of Skye and so didn't really hear what Father David had said in his address. He had read the twenty third psalm and the coffin had come in to 'Hey Jude' by the Beatles. It had been Marcus' favourite song for a while which Father David said was a sign of hope as St Jude was the patron Saint of lost causes. They had walked out listening to Gabriels Oboe from the film 'The Mission.' Her mother had sat rigid in her wheelchair. Only flinching when the curtains had closed and Marcus' body went on its final journey. His ashes were to be interred with those of his father in the crematoriums garden of remembrance. True to her word, Lara had been there sitting discreetly at the back with the young officer who had come with Ruth to search Marcus' room. It was pitiful and bleak and Eliza couldn't wait to get back to the house. There would be no wake. No glasses raised, no stories shared. Thirty four years on this earth and no one would miss him.

EDITH

It had been a better service than Edith had hoped. The vicar had read the psalm beautifully and spoken kindly of Marcus. Treasure in earthenware jars. Fragile. Breakable. We must try not to judge too harshly. She did try and she did still love the little boy he had been. If only he had never grown up.

She was exhausted and all her bones ached. Eliza had made an omelette for them both and they eaten in companionable silence. It would be her turn next to disappear behind the curtain and go down the schute in her coffin. She was ready. It would free Eliza up. She could sell the house and buy herself a little place. It was a shame really that she had come round after the attack. She had lived too long. The doctor had been to see her

139

yesterday. Nice comfortable sort of man. He had been around almost as long as her. He had asked her lots of questions which she had done her best to answer. He had suggested that maybe a residential nursing home would suit her better. Lots of people around. Activities, bingo even. She liked playing bingo, Eliza would come and see her and altogether it would be for the best. Give her a bit of life back. You've been stuck in this room too long Edith he had said. You could have a ground floor room there, look out the window and watch the birds. Even go out in the garden yourself if you would like to. Plenty of folks around to push your wheelchair. There are too many memories in this house. You need to breathe fresh air. Give yourself a chance. You've got time.

She had thought about it all night. She was just too tired though. Eliza wanted her to move she knew that. She hated the house. There had been laughter within its walls once. While they lived there though, there would never be again. Perhaps they were right. Perhaps it would be for the best.

TWENTY SIX

ELIZA

Doctor Forbes had come down in a serious mood after seeing her mother. "I don't need to tell you that she is deteriorating. Physically she is in pretty good shape all things considered. If she did more she would get stronger. Her heart is sound too. Mentally though she is much worse than when I last saw her. She is seriously depressed. She's confused and she is beginning to show signs of paranoia and I can't imagine that is going to improve. Marcus' death has pushed her over the edge. Guilt, regret, anger, they are all eating away at her. She's a strong woman and if she decides she doesn't want to go on she will gradually allow herself to die." "Can people do that?" Eliza had asked. "I have heard of people turning their backs to the wall but do people really make themselves die?"

" They can and they do." The doctor said softly

"I should never have moved away and left her. It was selfish selfish."

" Eliza Eliza , if you hadn't have left this house when you did, your mother would have been burying you too and that would have broken her heart. She needs a reason to go on, she needs a glimpse of something that she can grasp that will draw her out of the mire she is sinking in.

Residential care is my advice and if you both agree I can write up her notes and get the mental health assessment team round to see her. Sooner rather than later I would say. When are you going home?"

"I've got to go back Sunday ready for work on Monday. I'll come back every weekend for the moment until we can get something sorted. "

"Don't exhaust yourself will you? You are just beginning to break through from your own despair. There's a glint of life in your eyes now. You are sad and you are worried. You have carried too much for too long. Let it go. You can be free. Don't throw everything away now. Your mother wouldn't want that." Elizas eyes filled with tears.

" I've known you a long time. All of you. What happened affected us all. We just didn't know how to help. Seeing you so ill and not being able to even begin to touch your pain made me feel so helpless. You are stronger than you think Eliza. It is time for you to start believing that. Give me a ring when you have talked to your mother"

He picked up his bag and let himself out.

Eliza had gone up to her room and sat on the side of her bed. So much kindness. She sat and looked at the roses Ruth's twins had picked for her. Words started to form in her head and she got out her notebook.

I held the stillness as though it were a rose.
With care, with reticence, with beauty.
Silence welled deep within its petals
Far beyond the sweetest music
And I myself was held

As though a raindrop on the tip of a leaf
As though a child on the lap of one
Who is the music, and the rose , and the silence.
Most of all,
who is the silence.

Had she been held all these months and years? Could the memories of that night really not hurt her anymore?

It had been a Friday, just after seven. Marcus had been to a race meeting in Taunton and done pretty well. That wasn't why he was in high spirits though. That was because he was drunk. He had come up the stairs just as she had come out of the bathroom.

"Been waiting for me have you?" he had slurred at her.

"Waiting for the man of the house to come back and make a woman of you?"

She had tried to squeeze past him and get into her room, but he blocked her way. She pushed him away with as much authority as she could muster

"You're drunk Marcus now please get out of my way." She only had a thin blouse on and a wraparound and could feel the fear rising up in her. He mustn't know she was afraid though. She had to keep calm and be strong.

"Oh don't be like that Eliza" he had said suddenly grabbing her hair and pulling her closer to him. She could smell the sweat and the drink and thought she was going to be sick

"Let me go NOW`"

"Oh come on" he had said to her "we both know you want it. Been waiting a long time haven't you? Well todays your lucky day. " She had tried to scream but he put his hand over her mouth and pushed her to the floor at the top of the stairs. He was a heavy man and as hard as she tried she couldn't get him off her. Terror began to take over but as he pulled down her undewear and undid his zip she managed to scream NO NO

it didn't stop him forcing himself inside her. The pain was unbearable as he slammed her head against the floor all the time pushing deeper and deeper inside her until she thought she would pass out.

Out of nowhere their mother appeared. She had been out in the garden but heard Eliza's scream. Grabbing a kitchen knife she had run up the stairs and tried to pull Marcus off Eliza I'll kill you she had screamed, raising the knife above his head. Marcus had grabbed her wrist and as he had turned round to push her away they had both fallen down the stairs. The knife had gone into Edith just above her knee. The force of Marcus' weight on top of her had pushed it through the flesh until it could travel no further. She had hit her head on the wall at the bottom and been knocked unconscious. Thinking he had killed her. Marcus had fled. He had later been picked up in a bed and breakfast in Taunton. At the trial, not staying to help his mother had been the final nail in his coffin.

Eliza had crawled down the stairs and called an ambulance which took them both to hospital. Edith had remained unconscious for ten days and the damage the knife had done was so severe a surgeon had amputated her left leg the following day.

Much of what followed was a blur. The police interviews. The trial. She had found a way of transporting herself outside of her skin and looked on as though at someone else. She had showered and showered and showered but she couldn't get him out of her. His smell, everything about him infected her. She felt dirty. No filthy and there seemed nothing she could do to ever make herself clean again.

She had turned on her body. She stopped feeding it. She cut it with a razor blade. She hated everything about it and everything about herself.She felt guilty about what had happened to her mother and equally guilty about the hateful question that kept worming its way into her brain. Had she deserved it? Was it all her fault?

It was close to eight years now since that night. Had she really turned a corner? Was she stronger than she thought? Her mothers voice snapped her out of her trance.

Coming Mum. Coming.

EDITH

"I want to talk to you about my funeral." Edith said.

Oh mum haven't we had enough death can't it wait?".

"I'm serious I want you to write this down.

I'm not saying it wil be soon but it will happen one day. I don't want you to have to worry about anything when that day comes.

I would like psalm twenty three and psalm one hundred and twenty one. I want the reading where Jesus says let the little children come to me and music wise. All things bright and beautiful and The day thou gavest Lord has ended. Have you got that written down?"

Yes it's here Eliza had reassured her. Well just read it back to me so I know for sure.

Eliza had done as she was told which pleased Edith.

"You keep that bit of paper with you at all times do you hear?.

If I go into one of those homes things can go missing you know. People there won't know me. So it will be up to you to make sure it is all done right."

"Do you think you might give one of the residential homes a try?" her daughter had asked quietly

"Well. I'm thinking it might be a good idea don't you?

I'm not committing to it mind. Just testing the waters. If I don't like it I'm coming straight back here. "

"You don't have to rush anything mum. "

"Doctor Forbes mentioned I might be able to play bingo from time to time. That's not the only reason I'm going but it would be something to look forward to wouldn't it.?"

"It would. It would be fun and you never know you might win something."

"Exactly. Thing is Eliza. I don't want to die on my own. I am dying I know I am. I don't mind. I just don't want to go on my own."

"Doctor Forbes said your heart was strong and could keep going for years."

"Oh what does he know? He's past it. Asked me all sorts of stupid questions. His memory is worse than mine. He asked me what day it was. I mean you'd think a doctor would know wouldn't you? Otherwise how would he know which patients he was supposed to visit.?"

Ediths confidence suddenly evaporated. Her plan beyond her.

"We don't need to decide now do we? Lets sleep on it. Don't want to be too hasty. He said there was a garden there. So there might be a lot of bees. He didn't think about that did he eh?"

TWENTY SEVEN

ELIZA

It had been hard leaving her mother to return to Gloucester. Edith had no recollection of making the decision to give the home a try but Eliza went ahead and phoned Doctor Forbes all the same. A friend of his was going to help her negotiate her way through the process of gaining probate and they would take one step at a time with Edith.

She had gone back to work on the Monday to find a packet waiting for her.

Miss Eliza Harris c/o Gloucester Library Gloucester GL1

It came on Friday her boss had said. Thought about sending it on in case it was important but was worried it wouldn't get to you before you came back. Hope that was ok. By the way he had asked how did the funeral go? As well as it could she had replied. It was kind of him to ask. Niceties were so exhausting though.

Eliza put the packet in her bag vaguely curious but keen to get on with the work that took her mind off other things. It wasn't until she was on her lunch break that she opened it. It was a print out of a schedule of some sort and there was a card.

Dear Eliza

Hope this doesn't feel pushy or intrusive but I have printed out the From Couch to 5k timetable for you . Don't worry at all if you have decided it's not your thing! Sending you best wishes Pete.

A lump formed in Elizas throat. She flicked through the pages and read

WEEK 1

'For the runs in week one you will begin with a brisk five minute walk. Then you will alternate sixty seconds of running with ninety seconds of running for a total of twenty minutes'

She could do that couldn't she?

The card had a picture of two cheeky looking kittens on the front and she turned it over.

Card sold in aid of the RSPCA

She laughed. Really laughed and switched on the computer to access her emails.

Dear Pete
Thank you so much......

ELSEWHERE   .

As Eliza wrote her letter, another letter was being written this time from one of Her Majestys prisons. It was very short and very simple

Thank you. You done good.

The man writing it was the quiet non descript prisoner Marcus had shared a cell with for seven years. Stuart had listened to his companion whinge and whine about the injustice of his sentence and he had never said a word. A good listener he was.

He was in for stabbing a man to death. The man who had raped his niece. He still had two more years to serve but it didn't sadden him. He still had his pride and he still had a focus. He still too had friends on the outside. Friends he wrote to from time to time. Friends who like him thought rapists didn't deserve to draw breath. One of these friends, who happened to owe him a favour lived in Somerset and owned a black estate car.

SKYE

As the two letters were being written, hundreds of miles away on the Isle of Skye a solitary seagull was tossing sea weed around searching for food. When he was full, he stretched out his wings, tilted back his head and opened his beak. A haunting call as eternal as the mountains that stood behind him echoed out of the mist.